The Moving of the Water

the Moving of the Water

stories

David Lloyd

*for Sandy
in Ypsilanti
2018*

David

ee
excelsior editions

AN IMPRINT OF STATE UNIVERSITY OF NEW YORK PRESS

Cover art: Iwan Bala, *Cof, Bro, Mebyd* [*Memory, Community, Childhood*] (detail), 1997, oil on canvas.

Published by State University of New York Press, Albany

Excelsior Editions is an imprint of State University of New York Press

For information, contact State University of New York Press, Albany, NY
www.sunypress.edu

Book design, Aimee Harrison

Library of Congress Cataloging-in-Publication Data

Names: Lloyd, David T., 1954- author.
Title: The moving of the water : stories / David Lloyd.
Other titles: Moving of the water.
Description: Albany : State University of New York Press, 2018. | Series: Excelsior editions
Identifiers: LCCN 2017061603| ISBN 9781438472287 (paperback : alk. paper) | ISBN 9781438472300 (e-book)
Subjects: LCSH: Welsh Americans—Fiction. | Immigrants—United States—Fiction. | Welsh—United States—Fiction. | Utica (N.Y.)—Fiction.
Classification: LCC PS3612.L57 A6 2018 | DDC 813/.6—dc23
LC record available at https://lccn.loc.gov/2017061603

10 9 8 7 6 5 4 3 2 1

For my father
who told the first stories
R. Glynne Lloyd, 1909–1968

These stories are set in the Welsh-American community in Utica, NY during the mid-1960s.

Contents

Acknowledgments

Stories from this collection appeared in *Dodos and Dragons: An Anthology of Mauritian and Welsh Writing*, *The Lampeter Review*, *New Welsh Review*, *Stone Canoe*, *Third Wednesday*, and *Windmill*.

For advice and inspiration, I am grateful to John Bollard, Mike Jenkins, Patrick Lawler, Frank Lentricchia, Gareth Lloyd, Mair Lloyd, Margaret Lloyd, Nia Lloyd, Richard Lloyd, Chris Meredith, Linda Pennisi, and Patrick Scully. I could not have completed this book without the rigorous criticism and loving support of Kim Waale.

Rheinallt Llwyd generously provided guidance on characters' use of Welsh words and phrases.

Thanks to my editor James Peltz for his efficiency and encouragement.

Thanks to the Blue Mountain Center and the Hawthornden International Retreat for Writers for providing residencies where many of these stories were written and revised.

Now there is at Jerusalem by the sheep market a pool, which is called in the Hebrew tongue Bethesda, having five porches. In these lay a great multitude of impotent folk, of blind, halt, withered, waiting for the moving of the water.

—John 5:2–3 (King James Version)

Nos Da

WHY COULDN'T HE NAME IT? Something green. Unfamiliar. A good smell. Something green and . . . and something. He could smell another thing too, a bad smell without a name, damp and dark and close.

Lying on his back, he was staring at a sky bluer than any blue he could remember. Bluer than his father's eyes. Where are the clouds?

"Rich!" someone said, urgently, close to his ear. "It's me. It's Denny. Stay with me, buddy. You've got to stay with me. Tell me something. Your name. Start with that. Say your name."

Rich didn't say his name or look at Denny, squatting by his head. He heard a flutter in the distance, a bird's heartbeat. Can you hear a bird's heartbeat? The flutter didn't have a smell, not yet. It wasn't good, it wasn't bad. Like a basketball dribbled in a gym far away. Somewhere to his right, men were shouting, "Keep alert! Keep focused!" He didn't want to hear their voices. He wanted to hear the bird or the far away basketball.

Someone closer shouted, "Bowen! Private Bowen!"

Rich glanced at a big man kneeling by his legs. "State your name and rank!" the man shouted.

Rich had seen him before. Lambert. The medic. Sergeant Lambert. Rich shifted his gaze to the sky. He couldn't think of a reason to state his name and rank. "What's . . . that smell?" he asked Denny, croaking out the words.

3

"He's talking, Sarge," Denny shouted. "He's saying something."

Denny leaned close to Rich's ear. "Smell? I don't know. Don't everything smell like garbage in a garbage pit? But you're talking. It's great you can talk. Because as long as you're saying words, you're not, you know, not saying them."

"Like a thing you'd eat," Rich said. "But you wouldn't."

"Yeah, maybe," Denny said. "It's different here for sure. There's every stink you can imagine and plenty you can't. In a strawberry field, you smell strawberries. In a garbage dump, you smell garbage, and if it's not garbage, it will be." He sounded tired. "Anything I smell here, I wouldn't want to eat. Where the hell's that medevac, Sarge?"

"On its way."

"It needs to be here."

"I know," Lambert said. "I know. OK, got the tourniquets on."

"Can he feel anything?" Denny asked.

"Nah. Shock. And I pumped him with morphine."

The blue sky narrowed and darkened, though Rich didn't see clouds moving in. Strange to be here, he thought, and not somewhere else. Strange to hear a voice close, then far away. Strange to be on my back, staring at an empty blue sky, like staring at a ceiling while you're having your bath.

"When it's dark," Rich asked his father, sitting on the edge of his bed, "where does the sun go?" He was under the bedcovers, feeling warm, though his hair was damp from his bath. His bedside light illuminated his father's brown hair and white shirt, but the rest of the room was dark. He didn't want his father to leave—that's why he asked about the sun. If his father answered, Rich would answer his answer, and they'd be together longer. They would talk about where the sun goes. Megan was already sleeping. Their mother was putting away dinner dishes.

"It goes below," his father said. "No, sorry, it doesn't go any-where. We just can't see it. We turn away from it."

"Must be around three o'clock by now," Denny said. "They came out of nowhere, like shadows from under rocks. If shadows carried AK-47s. But now they're gone. The sun's out, the perimeter's secure, so they crawled under those god-damn rocks again with the snakes and spiders. Always coming and fucking going and fucking coming back again."

"Where does the sun go?" Rich said.

"Jesus," Denny said. "What is it now? The sun? I have no idea. I flunked astronomy, the most gut course you could take. That's why I'm here, I'm a flunky. The sun's far the fuck away is my guess. Other side of the earth. Like the dark side of the moon, you know?"

"A good smell," Rich said, "and a bad smell. That's what I don't get."

"What the hell's he talking about?" Denny asked Lambert, now working on Rich's left arm.

"No idea, but keep him talking. If he's talking, he's breathing. And if he's breathing, maybe he wants to do it some more. There, got the arm done. The medevac should get here any minute. Keep him talking, that's your job. I need to move on."

"OK, Rich, you know who I am, right?" Denny said, squeezing Rich's shoulder gently. "It's your buddy. Denny. Denny from Brooklyn with the six brothers and two sisters. Irish guy, remember? Good-looking—that's what Mom tells me. You stepped on a mine. I saw your foot go down and the earth go up. Then the gooks started firing, so it took a while to reach you. But Lambert, he's fast—you know, with what he does. And you . . . you'll be OK, I promise. You bought yourself a ticket home. No more freaking rice paddies. No holes in the ground to crawl into. No shadows in the daylight. Nothing more for you, buddy. You're all done. How you feeling?"

"Cold," Rich said. "The water gets cold."

"Yeah, it gets cold. It won't be long now, I promise."

"Dad was the one."

"For what?"

"For me. Friday nights."

"What? What was Friday night?"

"Bath."

"You liked that? God I hated bath night. Ed Sullivan and then a bath. But you couldn't enjoy the show, knowing what was coming next. The scrubbing, the stinging eyes. And if you're number seven in line, no hot water."

"Warm then cold. Then warm." Rich looked up at Denny. "Where's the towel?"

"Got no towel," Denny said. "I got nothing. I'm empty. Hey, I've got water." He lifted up his canteen. "You need water?"

"Cold."

"Yeah," Denny said. "You lost . . . you know, some blood. They've got blankets in the medevac. And coffee. It's a thousand degrees here, but I'd die for hot coffee. From Dominick's, Second Avenue. I'd actually die for that."

"She cried all night," Rich said. "And wouldn't get out of bed that morning."

"Who? Your girlfriend? I thought you didn't have a girlfriend. Hard to keep up with you, buddy. No moss under your feet. Don't matter what the girl wants. No one wants you to go. And you, especially. No one except your crazy Uncle Frank because he got sent to Korea and now thinks everyone should get an arm blown off like him. But here the fuck you are anyways. Talking, right? At least you're talking, and that's the main thing. Though I gotta be honest, I can't wait for the chance to shut up."

"Cars," Rich said.

"Now we're talking cars? Not many here. Unless you go to Saigon. What sort of wheels did you drive, anyway?"

"*Nos da*," Rich said.

"What?"

"*Nos da*." Rich was smiling.

"Are you talking Russian or something?"

"*Nos da*."

"That's not a car. What the fuck does it mean?"

"*Nos da*. Where does the sun go?"

"Fuck man, talk sense. I got no time for bullshit."

Rich again stared up at the blue sky, which had widened and brightened. He lifted his head to see himself. His legs were missing, but he could wiggle his toes. Just like in the bath, he could lift his feet and wiggle his toes. Lambert had cinched straps around his thighs. His fatigues were soaked dark red, but everything else was green: grass, leaves, trees, bushes—the hills were rolling, endlessly unfolding shades of green. Then the sky narrowed, leaving a pinprick of light. Rich wasn't sure if his eyes were closed or open or both or neither.

"Red," he said softly, "that's the bad smell. Green, that's the good smell."

Denny couldn't think of anything to say.

Now in complete darkness, Rich had a moment of certainty. He knew he was about to die.

"Chopper's here!" Denny shouted, standing and waving at the descending medevac churning up debris. The pilot in his massive helmet gave a thumbs-up.

"God-damn here at last! No more talking crazy bullshit. *You* are going *home*, Richie boy. Back to your cars and your fucking mother and father and girlfriend you maybe have and those baths you love and the sun on the dark side of the moon. Back to the towel. Nose-fucking-da, you crazy fuck. You're going home."

Key

LEWIS BOWEN was picking through a shoebox filled with a lifetime of odds and ends that belonged nowhere else. As a deacon of Bethesda Presbyterian he was entrusted with keys to the front door for emergencies when the sexton or Rev. Price couldn't be reached. He was sure he'd stored both keys in this box.

Lewis was alone in the kitchen. Megan had left with friends for the public library, researching a school project until the nine o'clock closing. What did she say? Something about World War I. Annie had gone to bed—it was only eight o'clock, but she went up every night after silently and robotically washing and drying the dinner dishes. Since Richard had been killed in Vietnam the previous May, she'd take three sleeping pills, drink a glass of apple juice, and sleep, motionless, hardly breathing until the alarm went off at seven the next morning. Lewis had spoken with Rev. Price about his wife's depression—but said nothing about his own increasing and perhaps blacker despair. Rev. Price advised that his wife become more involved with church and community activities. While getting her out of the house and interacting with people made sense to Lewis, she gave him blank stares or sharp words whenever he made a suggestion. "Involved," she said when he last brought up the subject. She repeated his word. "Involved. Involved. *In*-volved." She was making the word meaningless. "Involved with what, exactly?"

"With people. Church."

"Yes, of course. People. Church. Involved." And she made a noise that sounded like a laugh trapped in her throat. She stared at him then, as if the trapped noise should have made everything clear. She continued staring, grim and unblinking, until he at last turned from her.

Over the past few weeks he'd hardly spoken at all with his wife or daughter outside of what was necessary to move through the cycles of school, work, church, shopping, cleaning, eating, sleeping. He'd talk with his daughter over breakfast about what the day held for each of them, and when she'd left for school, he couldn't remember anything either had said.

Along with hairpins, broken watches, dead batteries, paperclips, and shoelaces tossed in over the years, the shoebox contained a number of keys. Where did they all come from? Lewis wondered. Had his family really needed to lock and unlock so many things? Spare keys to the Chevy he'd traded in two years earlier; skeleton keys to cabinets and doors around the house that, as far as he knew, had never been locked; keys to neighbors' houses; tiny keys that opened the jewelry boxes Megan had played with as a child, which had certainly been thrown away; and the key to a toy chest in which Richie had stored his model car collection, begun when he was six. Annie had tossed that collection in a black trash bag the day after the funeral, as she'd done with everything she associated with their son—clothes, books, toiletries, photographs, his basketball, his sneakers. Lewis tried to stop her, but she was manic and aggressively resolute, working from dawn to dusk filling bag after bag to expunge all that remained of her favorite child. But she'd forgotten about this key. Though it had nothing to fit into, Lewis was grateful for this proof that his son had existed, had lived with them in this house for eighteen years.

Annie had cried for days after Richie was drafted, and cried again, refusing to leave her bed, the morning he shipped off to

Vietnam, a place neither of them had heard of six months earlier. But she didn't cry when the soldiers in dress uniform arrived to tell them of his death. Didn't cry at his funeral or burial. And hadn't cried since.

And Megan? Silent, morose, secretive, she made hardly a ripple in their lives. They talked but didn't talk. Lewis had little idea what she did during the hours spent in her room after dinner behind a shut door. Not homework, as she claimed—her grades were just average, and her most recent report card was a mix of Cs and Ds. Once he stood for a quarter hour with his ear to her door but heard nothing, not even the soft crying he'd expected. Just silence. She went to occasional school dances and studied at the homes of girlfriends, though she hadn't brought a friend to their house since Richie had died.

At last Lewis found one of the two keys to the church—at some point Annie had tied a scrap of paper to it with the initials "BFD," Bethesda Front Door. He put on his heavy overcoat from the hall closet. Then he walked back to the kitchen and opened a bottom cupboard, removing a full pint of Canadian Club. He'd bought that pint for their big family Christmas dinner before Richie shipped out, but no one wanted any. He slipped it in his coat pocket. He stood still for a moment before walking slowly upstairs to the bathroom cabinet and taking out his wife's bottle of sleeping pills— it was half full. He put that in his pocket too.

IN THE DIM LIGHT he had trouble fitting the key into the front door lock. Once in, it turned easily. The heavy door shut soundlessly except for a quiet click. He hesitated in the darkness. He'd planned to walk through the narthex to the sanctuary, where some light might filter through the stained-glass windows, and he'd then stand before the cross. Ever since he was a child he had thought a cross—any cross—held an innate power. Now, this night, Lewis wanted desperately to feel that power—or at least to feel something that might move him in a new direction. Any direction, he thought, but the one in which he was headed. He stopped at the entrance to the nave. Though he peered in and strained his eyes, it was too dark to see the communion table and cross. Then it came over him fully and completely that nothing would happen in front of that cross—he'd sat before it every Sunday since Richie died. He'd prayed with his eyes fixed upon its polished brass on the oak communion table. It was hopeless—those high ceilings and the expanse of pews were no longer grand or even spiritual. They had become a space needing to be filled, but Lewis couldn't imagine what would fill it. He turned left, through a hall leading to a side chapel reserved for family gatherings before funerals or weddings. Lewis opened the door and stood a long time at the chapel entrance, allowing his eyes to adjust to the dark. It was a long, windowless rectangle with chairs lined up along one wall and a dozen pews in rows before a square altar, on which stood another, smaller, brass cross. He closed the door behind him.

Lewis carried a chair to a back corner of the chapel, as far from the cross as possible. When he felt his heart begin to race, he pulled the pint bottle from his overcoat pocket, unscrewed the top, and sipped, wincing from the burn down his throat. He'd never liked alcohol, and could rarely be persuaded to drink even a beer, but he'd heard that whiskey could give a man courage. People called the act cowardly. But the real cowardice, Lewis thought, was accepting a life of dulled pain, of moving through days and nights without touching, laughing, or even crying—as if simply existing had meaning or value. Just walking up and down stairs, opening and shutting doors—and never seeing what lay beyond. He knew that the ways he acted and felt—or couldn't act or couldn't feel—were damaging his daughter, and his wife, too. He'd become a poison in their systems. Every day they sipped a little more—and every day they died a little more.

The cross on the altar was a blur hovering in darkness, incapable of listening or speaking to him. He wasn't sure exactly when he'd stopped believing—it had been gradual, accumulative. One Sunday he couldn't bring himself to join the congregation in the Lord's Prayer. Another Sunday he'd wanted to laugh out loud when Rev. Price read the scripture lesson—about Jesus walking on the Sea of Galilee.

He sipped again, felt the same burn, set the bottle on the floor. He took out the pill bottle and shook it. A rattle like the rattle in his father's chest during those weeks before he died of emphysema in Faxton Hospital. Maybe like the rattle of blood in Richie's throat on the battlefield. What did that man write in his letter? The one who was with Richie? "Your son talked about you. 'Dad was the one.' That's what he told me before he died."

Then Lewis heard something. Voices. From where? Footsteps. The door opened, letting in light from a window beyond, and two figures walked past him and down the aisle, stopping half way to the cross. Strangely, Lewis didn't feel afraid, though he thought they must be burglars. Then, in the light through the open door, Lewis could make out a teenage boy and girl.

"I'll close the door," the girl whispered.

"No," the boy said. "I want to see your face."

The girl giggled. "OK, then."

They stood still, holding hands. Lewis knew it was Megan as soon as he heard her speak. The boy was tall, with dark hair. Lewis understood, now, that there was no World War I school project. Megan and the boy had arranged to meet at the library. She'd taken the second church key from the shoebox at some point—days, weeks, even months ago, hiding it in her room or maybe in that red purse they'd given her for her last birthday.

"Over here," she said.

They walked to the pew directly in front of the altar, and the ease and naturalness with which they moved in the dark made Lewis realize that this wasn't the first time they'd been here, secretly, by themselves. Maybe some weekend night when she'd told him she was going to a dance. Maybe some evening when she'd claimed she was seeing a movie with a friend. His daughter had created a life separate from his—with its own joys, terrors, and hopes, which he now glimpsed without permission. She'd created a life in this dark, windowless place with a boy Lewis had never seen before, whose voice he had never before heard.

Megan took off her coat and leaned back. The boy put his arm around her. Lewis saw their heads come together, heard their lips release. They began whispering. Hearing the rhythms of their intimacies made Lewis want to stand and shout out his daughter's name. Megan! She was *his* daughter. She belonged to him. She had lied to him. She had disrespected him and the church in which she'd been raised. A church, for God's sake. This church. She touched and kissed this unknown boy just a few feet from the cross. The anger surged through his body like electricity—then dissipated into the air.

Lewis felt weak and tired. A throbbing had begun at his left temple. Though his hands were shaking, he managed to screw the cap silently onto the pint bottle, slipping it into his coat pocket. He stood and crept to the open door. He paused to look over at the two heads still bent together, resting against the back of the pew, like a photograph removed from time, not anchored in place. He wondered if they would sense his presence. But they didn't.

Outside, the streetlights seemed to illuminate only circles in the air—not the sidewalk or Park Avenue or the dark church looming like a huge shadow overhead, and for a moment, Lewis wasn't sure which way to turn.

Visitor

MAE WILLIAMS liked her days to be organized. Nearing eighty, she couldn't do as much for herself as she wanted, so she allowed others to help, mostly women from church. In return, she'd babysit for them at no cost, as long as the parents brought the children to her apartment and picked them up. She rarely left the apartment— except to walk the one block to Bethesda Church. When her mother died at age eighty-nine, Mae moved from the house where they'd lived in Corn Hill to the small Elm Street apartment, though the neighborhood wasn't the best.

Most of her days revolved around church activities or occasional visitors arriving with her week's groceries or prescriptions for arthritis and high blood pressure or the few purchases needed to maintain her simple life—a radio when what she called her "wireless" finally broke and no parts could be found to repair it, light bulbs when the existing ones burned out, tissues when one of the boxes left around the apartment had been emptied.

The apartment was simply organized, modeled on the little terrace house in Llanberis in Wales where she'd grown up—a front parlor, small dining room, tiny kitchen and pantry, and two bedrooms, one of which she used as a sewing room. In Llanberis, her mother had fretted about how the parlor might look to passersby peeking through the front curtained windows from the street— which is why, during a period when her father was earning good wages in the slate mine, they bought a second-hand spinet and set

15

it opposite the window, though no one in the family could play it. They never allowed Mae to touch a key. But once, with both parents out of the house, she pressed a white key—and was surprised when it didn't make a sound. She pressed a black key—no sound. Then she struck the white key hard and heard something—a dull reverberation from deep within.

LEWIS BOWEN always walked Mae to the eleven o'clock church service, and she enjoyed his company. Lately, though, she'd been worried about him—since his son had died in that overseas war, he hadn't been himself. He looked shifty and skittish, as if he were hiding something. He'd stopped telling the jokes he used to try out on her—jokes Mae didn't understand, though she always laughed at what she took to be the punch line. She wanted to tell Lewis something that might comfort him. But she never did, hesitant to upset the routine they'd established.

Every Sunday after the service Lewis would walk Mae back to her apartment before rejoining his family. She'd have a few hours to herself then, before one of the deacons or elders would drive her to a parishioner's house for Sunday dinner. She knew they had organized a rotation so that no family would be too burdened—last week it was the Richards family, next week Mr. and Mrs. Parry. After dining with a succession of different families for eight or nine weeks, she'd find herself back at the first house. She hoped her hosts enjoyed her company. She couldn't talk about the politics of the city or the nation, or the new play at the Stanley, or modern books. She made what conversation she could—about Llanberis in her youth, or stories about her aunt and uncle and the fish-and-chips shop they kept in the village in the years when everyone spoke Welsh and went to chapel at least twice a week.

Mae was an only child, never married, so her experience was limited. Emigrating to America was the biggest thing ever to happen to her—she was nineteen, her mother thirty-nine, her father forty-one. She never owned a television—didn't enjoy that thing always talking in people's living rooms. She knew she repeated her stories, though no one except the youngest children ever pointed that out. Sometimes when the family hosting a Sunday dinner included teenagers, she would detect a smirk or a giggle at her expense. The father or mother would frown sternly—and the offending children would stare at their plates until finally released to the TV. She didn't mind, not really, and she hoped they weren't punished after she'd left. She'd been young too, once, and knew that old people could seem like creatures from another world. There were, of course, stories that she didn't tell. About drunk Uncle Robert deliberately making her mother cry during Christmas dinner when she was twelve. Or, worse, about Geraint bringing flowers the day he proposed, talking to her parents in the parlor, behind a shut door, while Mae sat alone at the kitchen table.

After everyone had finished tea and dessert, Mae would be driven back to her apartment, when she'd have a few hours to prepare for babysitting—she only accepted children between the ages of seven and ten. If they were very young, they made Mae nervous—she was too old to chase them, and fearful that they might fall and hurt themselves. And if older than ten they might become bored and unhappy, staring out the window even when asked direct questions. But children between seven and ten generally laughed when she laughed, did as they were told. And they liked card games, so they would help Mae set up a card table in her dining room with cookies and juice, and she and the children would play Pennies from Heaven, Old Maid, or Canasta until eight o'clock, when the parents would arrive. The only time she ever felt a bit annoyed was when parents were late. They'd apologize, and she'd insist that it didn't matter. But she thought they should not presume that she had nothing to do of an evening except care for their children.

MAE OPENED THE DOOR TO see Twm Kendrick, in tan trousers and white shirt, holding a black gun, finger on the trigger, the long muzzle pointed at Mae.

"A present for his ninth birthday," the boy's father said. "He's been asking for a machine gun since he saw one on TV—what was it Twm? Four months ago?"

"Al Capone had it," the boy put in.

"And now," the father continued, "he won't go anywhere without the ghastly thing. Do you mind? It doesn't shoot bullets, and it won't make any noise."

Mae said she didn't mind, if it was just a toy.

Mr. Kendrick laughed a little too loudly. Twm scowled. She could see his finger lightly flicking the trigger.

"Now, Twm," Mr. Kendrick said, putting a hand on the boy's head, "you must mind Miss Williams. Do exactly as she says. Sling the machine gun over your shoulder using the strap, as I showed you. You won't lose it that way. And remember what we talked about: no pinching, no biting. Do you understand?"

Twm nodded. Mae noticed that the boy now aimed the muzzle at his father.

"Good. I'll be back by eight." Mr. Williams gave Twm a little push towards Mae. "I'm sure he'll be no trouble."

When Mr. Kendrick had left, Mae told Twm she would give him a tour of her apartment. She planned to finish in the kitchen, where she would offer *bara brith* with butter. She hoped he would then put his machine gun down, and they could start a card game.

"Here are my parents," she told him, pointing to a framed portrait of a grim elderly couple, dressed in black. "I always begin my tour with them. When that photograph was taken they were younger than I am now. Can you imagine that? They were more old-fashioned even than me."

"You can't see that man's mouth because of his mustache," said Twm. "How did he eat?"

"Oh, like the rest of us," Mae said. "Though he used his napkin more often."

"Are they dead?" Twm asked.

"My father passed away in nineteen forty-eight, bless him. My mother two years after that."

Twm examined the photograph carefully. "They don't look nice," he said. "They look as if they don't give presents."

"Oh, no," Mae replied. "They certainly . . . well they certainly were . . . nice in their way."

Next to the photograph was a glass vase of small purple flowers. Twm slung the machine gun over his shoulder. "What are these?" he asked. He touched a petal.

"Primroses. A bouquet of primroses. Don't they smell wonderful?"

Twm sniffed, and shrugged his shoulders. "Mother's Day was last week."

"They're not for Mother's Day, dear."

"Then why?"

"Well, they're pretty, aren't they?"

"But why?"

"They're from a friend."

"Did your boyfriend give them?"

Mae was startled by the question. "I was thinking we might play a card game tonight," she said. "I love cards. Have you ever played Pennies from Heaven? Or Canasta?"

"Old Maid!" the boy shouted, a crafty look in his eyes. "I want to play Old Maid!"

"Certainly," Mae said. "We could."

"My dad says if you had a boyfriend, he'd be older than you and probably dead."

"Oh, my goodness," Mae said. She dropped onto the parlor couch.

"If you had a boyfriend, how come you didn't marry him?"

Mae was staring at the vase of flowers.

After a quick glance at Mae, Twm grabbed the bouquet from the vase with both hands, and ran from the parlor.

"Twm!" Mae called from the couch. She saw a trail of water drops and a few primroses along the carpet, which she followed to her bedroom. A black muzzle poked out from under the bed.

"Twm," Mae said, "I know you're hiding beneath the bed. You must come out."

"I got a hostage," he said. He thrust out the bouquet, gripped by the stems, and yanked it back under. "So don't try anything funny."

"Please give me the flowers," Mae said. "They're important to me."

"Why?"

"We can set up a card table in the dining room," she said, without much conviction.

"Why are the flowers important to you if you don't have a boyfriend or he's dead? Why aren't they just flowers that don't smell much?"

Mae returned to the front parlor. She stared at the photograph of her parents and the empty vase. She sat on the couch, tugged a handkerchief from her sleeve and began to softly cry.

Twm appeared in the doorway, walked to the vase, and stuffed the bent, disheveled primroses back in. He spread them out, drooping and twisted.

"Good as new," he said.

He aimed his machine gun at the photograph of Mae's parents, and pressed the trigger. "Rat a tat a tat a tat," he shouted. "Rat a tat a tat a tat a tat a tat a tat." He looked over at Mae. "Stop crying," he told her. "I didn't kill the hostage. The hostage is OK, see?" He pointed his gun towards the primroses. "I killed the bad people."

"I see."

"I did that for you," he said. "I felt sorry for you."

Mae said nothing.

"I said, 'I did that for you.' Did you hear?"

"It's too late," she said.

"Why?"

Mae wiped her eyes one last time and slipped her handkerchief up her sleeve.

"Can I have something to eat?" Twm lowered the muzzle. "I'm hungry."

"Hungry?" Mae sounded bewildered. "For food?"

"I'm starving. I'm always starving."

"I have *bara brith* in the kitchen."

"My Nain made that before she died. She was like you, skinny. Skinny as a rail, my dad says. Do you have milk to go with it?"

"Yes."

"OK."

"I HOPE HE WASN'T TOO MUCH TROUBLE," Mr. Kendrick said when Mae opened the door.

"He's certainly a handful," Mae said.

"Two hands," he replied. "Sometimes three."

Twm stood behind her, machine gun slung on his shoulder, arms stiff at his sides, staring straight ahead. "I'm not going home," he announced. "I'm staying with this old lady. She needs me."

"Of course you're coming home," Mr. Kendrick said. "Your mother's waiting in the car. We're leaving right now. And don't refer to Miss Williams that way. It's rude. Now, what did you and Miss Williams do tonight? No pinching I hope. And of course, no biting."

"First I had to kill bad people."

"Certainly you did. Bad people sometimes need to be killed." He winked at Mae. "What an imagination. Isn't he something else? I only wish it could translate into decent grades at school. Or at least decent behavior." He returned his attention to Twm. "After killing the bad people what did you do? Did you bury them? Did you have a funeral? Did you say a prayer?"

"We ate raisin bread, then played Old Maid. I won, she lost."

"Did she? Did she indeed? Miss Williams, if you don't mind me asking, is that true? You played a card game with Twm?"

Mae cleared her throat softly. "Yes, it's true."

"You have quite the way with children, Miss Williams," he said, nodding his head in admiration. "I think Twm will want to visit with you again."

IN HER BEDROOM, Mae removed from the closet the one elegant dress she owned—a flouncy, joyful purple, reaching almost to her ankles but hanging loosely over her humped shoulders and boney hips. She put on the dress and brushed her thin, gray hair with quick strokes. She fastened a string of pearls around her neck. She slipped on the shoes she'd worn to church that morning. In the bathroom she applied lipstick sparingly—one tube could last the better part of a year. The church women must have been surprised when lipstick appeared on her shopping list. They'd never seen her wear any in church—or on any occasion.

At nine o'clock the doorbell rang, as it always did. And as always, Mae walked slowly to answer it, savoring each step. She opened the door to a familiar face—Geraint, with a bouquet of primroses, which she accepted with a bow of thanks. After she arranged them in a vase by her parents' photograph, the two sat side by side on the couch and talked—in Welsh of course—about the village in which they both grew up. They told each other stories. She spoke about her favorite cousin who'd died near the end of the First World War. He spoke about his parents, Ifor and Eluned, and the terrible years after his father lost his job because of the miners' strike. As he spoke, she admired his soft, brown curls, his earnest expression. She never felt as if she were repeating her stories, and Geraint always seemed interested.

He'd end the visit the same way each time. "I must be going," he'd say, glancing at his pocket watch—a watch she suspected he wore only for these visits. "I've kept you long enough."

"Oh, dear me," she'd say. "I feel as if you just arrived. But yes, it is late, isn't it? Almost ten. How does time go by so quickly?"

"How indeed?" he'd reply, and then he'd stand.

She'd walk him to the door. In the hallway he'd turn and ask the two questions he always asked at the conclusion of his nightly visit.

"Why did you leave? Did you really have to leave?"

And she'd say, "Yes. I did, you know. I was only a girl. Just a village girl."

"Oh no," he would say. "You were far more than that."

"I had to do what they told me to do. I had no choice. They didn't give me a choice."

And that's when he'd look at her fully, openly.

"I had written it out you know, everything I wanted to say so I wouldn't make a mistake. About the job at my uncle's grocery on the high street. Everything. It was your mother who objected, more than your father. Your mother."

She'd blush, feeling her face prickle.

"And if they had to leave, I wish they had let you stay," Geraint would say next. "In the village with me. Or at least in Wales."

"But you were happy enough," Mae would say. "You married, didn't you? You raised a family. You had a good life in the village."

"Yes," he'd say. And he'd say nothing for a moment. "I did marry. I had a family. But, you know . . ."

At that point she'd stop him. "Please," she'd say, "we mustn't. This has been such an agreeable visit." She didn't want the evening to turn sad. Not after such pleasant conversation.

That was all the urging he'd need. He'd smile, bow his head, and leave her, walking down the hallway, disappearing as completely as if he'd never been there at all.

Crooked Pie

"JACOB!" his mother called. "I'm having a word with Mrs. Richards, but we'll be along shortly. Keep close to your brother, and don't stray."

"Keep—Close—Don't—Stray." One word per step. Jake watched one sneaker hit the ground with each word. His mother behind, his brother and David ahead, him in the middle, with one word per step. "Keep—Close—Don't—Stray."

What does it mean to stray? he wondered. Is it a cat in an alley? Is it Hansel and Gretel and the gingerbread house?

And what does it mean to keep close? Is that a shoelace in a sneaker? Or a foot in a sock? Or the ring on Mam's finger? Dad didn't wear a ring. "Welshmen don't," he'd said, when Jake once asked about it. Then his dad held up his hand and made a fist. Four knuckles, four fingers, a thumb curled behind, but no ring. "See?" he'd said. "See what I mean?"

His mother's ring was yellow. But too yellow, Jake thought, like egg yolk.

Jake, his mother, his older brother Peter, and Mrs. Richards with her son David had walked across the rusted drawbridge over a dry, shallow moat into Play Land of the Adirondacks. Now they were continuing to the Emerald Forest. It was late on a Saturday afternoon, so most visitors were heading back towards the exit and the parking lot.

Peter and David—both thirteen—whispered to each other, glanced back at Jake, and took off running down the cobblestone path. Jake knew where they were headed: to Ali Baba's Cave, not a cave at all but a labyrinth inside a fake mountain with a low, dark entrance. It could be ninety degrees outside, but when you stepped into this place it was always cold—a windowless interior dimly lit by exit lights and smelling vaguely like a locker room. Here and there, urns and open treasure chests showed glittering rocks, fake jewels, and over-sized gold coins—everything glued in place, though gaps and gouges showed where some had been pried loose and pocketed. Shadowy rooms and passages led off the main hallway—once, Jake saw an older boy and girl in an alcove, her shoulders pressed against the wall, his hands on her hips, thumbs hooked onto her belt as if it belonged to him. Jake hated Ali Baba's Cave ever since the summer when Peter and David jumped him in the Harem Hideaway, shouting that they were "Ali Baba's forty thieves." Peter straddled Jake's chest while David peeled off his sneakers and socks and ran away. When David returned, he said he'd stuffed them down an urn but wouldn't say which of the hundred plastic urns scattered through the labyrinth. In the nearest, Jake found a boy's soiled underwear. In another, he caught the bitter stink of piss.

"Jacob!"

Jake kept walking, staring at the rise and fall of his sneakers.

"Jacob Meredith! Did you hear me?"

He stopped. "Yes."

"Why didn't you answer?"

Jake shrugged.

"I don't like your attitude, young man," she said. "Acting as if you're all by yourself without regard to anyone. And who do you think you're meant to be?"

"No one."

"All right then. Catch up to Peter and David right now. You boys must stay together."

WHEN OUT OF HIS MOTHER'S SIGHT, Jake saw that the main path, sign-posted Ali Baba's Cave, continued on, while a narrower path on the left led to Story Book Village: Where Magic Rules. Jake had been down that path before and remembered the houses of Sleeping Beauty, Goldilocks, Red Riding Hood, Cinderella, Snow White. He'd been inside each—too many times. After walking past a big red trash can overflowing with plastic cups and green French fry baskets, Jake stopped before a house he didn't remember—The House of the Crooked Old Man—which looked like nothing else in the Forest. It must be new, Jake thought, though it didn't look new or old, just different. The roof was longer on the left than the right, the chimney was a melted oval, the windows were trapezoids. On the front door hung a plaque with a nursery rhyme in gothic lettering:

There was a crooked man who walked a crooked mile
and found a crooked sixpence upon a crooked stile.
He bought a crooked cat, which caught a crooked mouse,
And they all lived together in a little crooked house.

When you stepped inside any house in Story Book Village you saw a life-size plaster character from a fairy tale. In the House of the Three Bears, a pouty girl with golden curls sat in an oversize armchair eating porridge, her big, brown spoon held between the bowl and her open mouth. In Snow White's House, a dark-haired girl leaned over a huge pot hung above a mound of rocks painted red—pretending to be a fire. She was staring at it, wide-eyed, as if it wasn't a pot but a crouching animal. Or maybe what was in the pot amazed her—concrete painted brown, a soup, Jake guessed, with big hard bubbles that would never burst. The most enticing of all was Sleeping Beauty's House—you walked through the front door directly into a bedroom. The whole house was one big bedroom, with chests of drawers, mirrors, and little tables set against each wall. No bathroom, kitchen, or TV room. In the middle, a double bed looked comfy but felt as hard and cold as the concrete it was made of. On the bed, Sleeping Beauty slept in a low-cut, frilly deep blue nightdress, surrounded by plaster teddy bears, her lips as red as fresh blood, her face as white as a stick of chalk, her blond hair draped over her shoulders and bare arms, her eyes shut tight. She held a rose between her breasts—and seemed altogether as helpless, Jake thought, as a baby bird in a nest. Below her head on the concrete pillow, someone had drawn an erect penis in red lipstick. The first time Jake saw that, he tried to rub it off with his sleeve, but the red had seeped into the concrete and was embedded in the display. He wondered why the people who took care of Story Book Village never bothered to paint over it.

The Crooked House was altogether different: here a bald man stood in the front yard—not inside the house. He wore a lime-green jacket with acorns for buttons, an orange tie, a forest-green vest, and bright red pants, all freshly painted. One shoulder humped half a foot above the other, legs and elbows bent at sharp angles, eyes uneven, irregular protruding cheekbones. Even his smile was crooked—normal on one side, weirdly downward-sloping on the other. "Come in, young man!" he seemed to be saying. "Let me offer you a slice of delicious crooked pie!" Jake liked that the house was run by a man, not a woman. A man who looked nothing like his father. This crooked man had big oval rings glued onto his fingers and thumbs—all painted gold, though some paint had chipped off. The expression on his face reminded Jake of Taid, his mother's father, who'd died last fall. At night Taid would read to Jake in Welsh from a Bible as Jake listened and nodded at the flow of language, not understanding a word. Taid's hands were so knotted from arthritis that Jake had to turn the pages whenever Taid raised his crooked finger.

The first room of the Crooked House contained familiar objects that were also somehow unfamiliar: a clock with thirteen numbers, a chair with a seat that tilted sharply left, a framed painting of the crooked man in the same pose as the plaster statue outside, displaying the same crooked smile. It's all different here, Jake said to himself. Everything looks old and new all at once. You can't tell time. The floor was crooked too, with a peak in the middle, so you had to walk up then steeply down to reach the door to the next room. To the right of that door a cat with bent ears sat on its haunches. And in the cat's mouth, a crumpled mouse with zigzag whiskers. You might feel sorry for the mouse until you looked into its squinty, nasty eyes.

The door opened soundlessly into the strangest sight in the house—a completely normal bedroom, with a rectangular chest of drawers, a symmetrical oval mirror, and a desk and chair by the wall that could have been in Jake's own bedroom. It was so normal, after all the crookedness in the other room, that it felt alien and uncomfortable to Jake. And the most uncomfortable thing of all was a teenager sitting on a narrow bed smoking a real cigarette, staring out the back window—the only window in the room. A real teenager. He turned towards Jake, wrinkling his nose, as if smelling something bad.

"Oh," Jake said. "Sorry. I'm really sorry."

"What for?" The teenager took a drag, exhaling a blast of smoke. "It's a free country, last I heard."

"I didn't know anyone was here."

"So now you know. Someone's here."

Jake turned to leave but the boy called out, "Wait a sec! What's your name?"

"My name?"

"Don't you have a name? Most people do."

Jake hesitated, not knowing if he should say his name. Was it straying if you said your name to someone you didn't know? Wasn't there a story in which someone told someone his name and then stomped his foot through the floor and died?

"Jake," he said. "I'm Jake."

"Get out of town!"

"What?"

"That's my name. *I'm* Jake, not you. Get yourself in here. If you took my name, I need to ask you something."

Jake stepped into the room and immediately felt like turning and running. But he stood still. "Ask me what?"

"How old are you?"

"Me?"

"Yeah, you. See anyone else in here? Am I missing something? Is someone hiding under this bed?"

"I don't think so."

"Then tell me how old you are."

"Ten. Almost eleven."

"Well that's goddamn weird. I'm fifteen, almost sixteen. If you divide your age in half and add ten, you get my age exactly. Doesn't that blow your mind?"

"Yeah," Jake said. "I guess."

"So we're, like, cousins. Better than that, I'm your older brother." He flicked ashes to the floor. "So ask me something. Anything. It's your one chance. After me, alls you got is yourself, and all anyone will tell you will be bullshit."

A rash of acne flowed across the teenager's cheeks and forehead, and greasy black hair hung to his eyebrows and covered his ears. A sparse mustache shadowed his upper lip.

"I already got a brother," Jake said. "And I should go find him."

"Ask me something first."

"How come this room is normal and the rest of the house is all crooked?"

"Because I'm in it is why. But that's a dumb question. Don't you want to know about life? About what's down the road? If it's a car accident or a convertible with a key? Ask me a real question."

Jake wouldn't ask because he thought a real question might get him in trouble.

"OK, I see the problem. You're clueless. That's OK. I used to be clueless, too. And then, guess what? I found out who done it."

"I need to find my family."

"What's the rush? I don't hear anyone calling your name. I don't hear anyone shouting 'Jake! Hey, Jake, where the heck are you? We miss you! Come on home to mommy and daddy!' So how come you're here by yourself? What's the deal?"

Jake shrugged.

"I'm by myself, too." He dropped and stepped on his cigarette. "That's my deal."

"Why?" Jake asked.

"It's a good place to be when you're sick of where you are. Tomorrow I'm going somewheres else, far from this shit hole." He ran fingertips over the inflamed disks on his cheek.

"Where's that?"

"Someplace not here, like I said. So where are you? Right now I mean."

"Me? Here, I guess."

"Where do you live is what I'm asking."

"Utica."

"Jesus, man, you're bullshitting me," the teenager said. "That's my city. Whereabouts in Utica?"

"Holland Avenue."

"The city end?"

"Near the cemetery."

"Yeah, well, same difference. In a few years you'll be on the move, like me. There's a world out there, you know? People doing things you can't talk about because you've never seen them. Things kids get into. Haight-Ashbury's where I'm headed. Soon as I find a road going west I'm sticking out my thumb. You stand still or you move, that's how it is. There's no in between, not unless you're dead. Then you just... fall down because your legs don't work. Right? Do you want to find yourself in Vietnam all fucked up in some place you can't pronounce, waiting for someone to pack up your body parts?"

"No."

"That's what I'm saying. That's down the road. But me, I'm *on* the road—and I'm not stopping 'til I see the sign for Haight and the sign for Ashbury."

"What about your family?" Jake asked.

"Like my brother gives a shit. Like my mother cares. Like Dad knows if I'm eating Fruit Loops or Cheetos at the breakfast table— the bowling team's more his thing, know what I'm saying? You gotta be a Moose or an Elk, not a human. But this is America, that's the thing. This is where bullshit changes. And that's what I'm gonna do, change the bullshit, move the bullshit to somewheres else."

"My dad bowls," Jake said. "Three times a week."

"Tell me about it," the older boy said. "The Pin-O-Rama on Oneida Street, right? Your mom buys toothpaste at Daw's Drugs and socks at the Boston Store. Tell me my story. All the goddamn words no one says. All the somebodies you're supposed to be just because they're like somebody you never met who died across the ocean."

"I like where I live," Jake said. "I don't need change."

"That's because you're ten. Divide that in half, add it to your age, and you're me. Like it or not, and I'm guessing not. You'll get older, like me. You'll get zits on your face. You'll start seeing girls. Girls will see you, yeah, even your skinny self with those zits and all your cluelessness. They'll look at you and want you to look back and you'll die of looking because that's all it is. No touching involved. And your parents won't go away, right? They're all about where they came from, which is where you're supposed to go. They'll be in the bathroom or the kitchen, in your face or behind your back, acting as if your life is theirs. You keep pouring water into those radiator pans on Saturdays, don't you? You keep walking the dog when the dog just wants to sleep. And one day you'll do something to your brother so shitty bad in the alley behind that downtown Woolworth's, he can't ever forget. You'll have arguments with your mom and dad. They're all about themselves, right? Themselves, and who grows the best shrubs. And you got to trim those shrubs. That's your job. You got to work those shears every Saturday. They might pay you a quarter, maybe fifty cents. Even if they're dead and brown. Even if you hate shrubs. And that fifty cents goes to your college savings account. Do they listen to what you say?"

Jake shook his head.

"Believe me, there's gonna be shouting. Time goes on, don't it? You'll go to a dance at your ugly-ass brick school gym and lean against the wall. You'll play bumper pool at the downtown Y because nothing else is happening. You'll smoke cigarettes in that lot behind the museum, sitting on a curb. You'll drink Utica Club with friends in Murnane Field, hiding the can under your jacket, and your parents will be like, 'That's the devil's drink' when it comes off your breath. They'll make you confess your sins at two in the morning. You'll listen to rock and roll in your best friend's basement. You'll dry hump like crazy on somebody's lumpy couch. And you can. Because this is America. It's what kids are doing. And you're smart, I see that. You're smarter than them. They're stuck in history, with houses made of stone, right? In places with names you can't pronounce. Am I right? As fucked up as this fucked-up house. But you're not here. You're in the future. You've been reading about California. San Francisco. You know about napalm don't you? How skin melts off a body? You've been listening to records everyone older than you hates. You've been reading books your parents want the library to throw on a bonfire. So what do you do? You go to the kitchen like you're getting a glass of milk. Instead you take money from the cookie jar and walk out the front door. You stick out your thumb. You head west. You want to live your life, cause no one else is gonna do it if you don't. And if they did, it would suck and you'd fall down and die."

"Don't stray," Jake said. "Stay close."

The teenager stood from the bed. A blotchy, reddish flush had spread from his face to his neck.

"I'm not bullshitting you," he said. "It's the truth. It's Truth or Consequences. And you better get ready."

Then the door behind Jake opened to reveal his mother and behind her, Peter and David. Further back in the crooked living room, Jake glimpsed Mrs. Richards' frowning, pasty face. For a confused moment he thought the witch from the Gingerbread House had joined them.

"Where have you been?" his mother demanded. She stepped into the bedroom, taking hold of Jake's arm. "We've been all over Play Land looking for you! We went to every house in the Village. You've worried me sick."

"You're hurting me!" Jake shouted, yanking his arm away.

"That's nothing compared to what your father will do," his mother said. "He only needs an excuse."

No rings on any fingers, Jake thought.

Jake's brother squeezed by his mother into the room. "We waited for you in the cave," he said. "A long time we waited because we had something to tell you. And here you are, in the stupidest room there is."

"What on earth are you doing here?" his mother asked. "Alone in this place?"

"I'm not alone," Jake said. "And it hasn't been that long." He turned, but the teenager was gone. And everything that was previously straight and normal now looked crooked.

"There was a guy here," Jake said. "He talked a lot. He knew a lot."

"I don't care who was here," his mother said. "You should have stayed with your brother. You can't leave us and go somewhere no one knows about." She crossed her arms and waited, but Jake said nothing.

"You'll never do this again, do you hear?" she said.

She pulled Jake roughly from the bedroom into the crooked living room, past the frowning Mrs. Richards and her son, out to Story Book Lane. When she let go, his arm ached, and he was angry at being treated like a toddler in front of Mrs. Richards, her son, and his smirking brother.

"Follow me," his mother said. "We're going to the car right now, with no more foolishness."

And they all started down Story Book Lane, his mother and Mrs. Richards leading the way, Peter and David next, with Jake at the rear.

Jake looked back at the crooked man with his cue ball head and stupid clothes, and all the fake rings on his fake fingers and thumbs.

"Come into my house young man!" the eyes seemed to be saying. "Let me offer you a slice of delicious crooked pie!"

Eeeeeee!

BEN WATCHED THE MAN'S EYES dart wildly left and right. Lumpy—Lumpy Lombardi—and Ben and Sal were in Lumpy's office in the Ace of Hearts nightclub on James Street. The room had a desk, a chair, a phone, and a plush maroon rug, so it could be called an office, but the wet bar fronted by six black vinyl stools, the bare light bulb fixture in the ceiling, and the pin-up girl posters on the walls gave a different impression.

Lombardi was duct-taped to the chair. With tape also wound around his mouth, he could only beg for mercy with grunts and moans. The single word Ben thought he understood was *please*, which came through as a long vowel, a plaintive *eeeeeee*. Lombardi's sweet cologne mixed with his sour body odor, producing a skunkish stink that filled the room.

"*Eeeeeee.*" Lombardi screeched out the sound, eyes fixed on Ben's gun. "*Eeeeeee. Eeeeeee.*" He sounded like a wounded bird.

"ALL YOU DO IS POINT THE PIECE," Sal had told Ben earlier that day in the back room of Sal's nightclub, the Piccadilly Lounge on Bleecker Street. Ben sat on the leather couch, Sal was perched on the edge of his desk. "You're the muscle, so you point the piece and scare the be-fucking-Jesus out of that scumbag. Can you do that for me? Can you handle that?"

"Yeah, I can handle that."

"You know why I chose you for this job?"

Ben shrugged. "Not really."

"Because I've had my eye on you. You don't give any fucking attitude. You do as you're told and keep your mouth shut. And you're not related to anyone."

"No," Ben said, "I'm not."

"All right," Sal said. "All right, big guy. Here it is." Sal opened a desk drawer and with a pocket handkerchief removed a small black revolver. "You can use this, right?"

Ben took the gun. "Yeah."

"And give it back when you're done."

"Sure."

Sal raised his thick black eyebrows. "That's a joke," he said. "Because if you don't give it back you get stuffed down a well in Frankfurt, know what I mean? It's a hundred dollar piece. Completely clean. Is today your goddamn birthday or something?"

"No," Ben said. "It's not my birthday."

"All right. Good. This is a test. Don't blow it. I'm counting on you not to blow it, OK?"

"OK."

"If you do good, there's more of this work for you. Maybe someday that piece'll be yours for real because I've had my fill of goombas fucking up and expecting a pass because they married my second cousin Mona, you know? You heard about that one, right?"

"Yeah, I heard," Ben said, though he had no idea what Sal was talking about.

THE WHOLE POINT OF THE JOB was to scare Lombardi into telling Sal a name. That's what Sal had told Ben in the Pic: "We just need the name. He'll cave. He'll give it up. Then we leave. We do it, and it's over."

Up to this point everything *had* been easy. He and Sal had surprised Lombardi in the bathroom attached to his Ace of Hearts office. Ben pulled out the gun, and Lombardi—who looked so tough at six feet four and three hundred pounds, with slate-gray, wavy hair slicked back from his pockmarked face (hence "Lumpy")—this tough guy yanked up his boxer shorts and started bawling: "Don't shoot, don't shoot, I'll make it up Sal, I promise. What d'you need? Money? Girls? I got new girls, just hired, I promise. Spanking new, know what I mean? How 'bout a drink? Let's have a drink on me, OK? Got lots of top-shelf shit. Think about my Darlene. We got two kids, don't we? Let's not do something we'll regret. Just tell your man to put the gun away and . . ."

Sal told Lombardi to shut the fuck up—about Darlene and everyone else in his soon-to-be-nothing world, and anyway didn't he know Joey Mustache had fucked Darlene on this very desk a month ago, no lie? While Ben aimed the gun at Lombardi's face, Sal sat him at his desk chair with his pants around his ankles, duct-taped his wrists together, taped his mouth while he was still pleading for mercy, then taped his massive hulk to the chair—using an entire roll of duct tape. Sal removed the money from Lumpy's wallet and twisted a gold ring off his pinky.

"Sal," Ben said. "Why'd you tape his mouth?"

"So he can't fucking scream. You want to hear this loser scream? Is that music to your ears?"

"But . . . you know?" Ben wasn't sure how much to say. "You need that thing. We're here to get that thing. So . . . he needs his mouth."

Ben didn't know why Sal needed Lumpy to tell him a name. He didn't know what the person the name belonged to had done to Sal, or to someone higher up than Sal, or why Lombardi was the only one who could give the name. He only knew that this was his first real job, and a dozen guys in East Utica would give an index finger to work for Sal Ruggerio. Ben's other jobs for the last three years had been petty cash pick-ups or small-time burglaries or just standing outside a locked door in a building where something was happening—though no one ever told him what, dice or girls or drugs or important people making decisions. It was a life of slumming for nobodies who worked for somebodies who worked for Sal. Working for Sal directly made Ben somebody. Ben had never been somebody, not when he lived with his parents on Briar Avenue when he first got to know the Italian kids in his neighborhood, not when he went to Bethesda with his parents every Sunday, not when he left his nothing neighborhood to move in with Ray and Moose in East Utica. This was his chance to break out. But now Ben was nervous—the job was taking too long, and Sal wasn't focused.

"Maybe he could write the name," Ben said, "but not with his wrists taped. You know, together like that."

Sal tossed the wallet on the floor.

"Looks like burglary, don't it, Lump?" he said. "A bullshit burglary is all this is. With damage on the side. The cops in this town understand damage on the side. Like Scalzo's boy, remember? What a monumental fuck-up that was."

Lombardi grunted a few words, ending with that long *eeeeeeee.*

"Sal," Ben said. "Shouldn't you get the name so we can go?"

But Sal was still talking to Lombardi. "I'm glad we shared this time," he said. "Because you and me, we're Bleecker Street brothers, right? Joey Mustache's boys, back in the day. Had some fun, didn't we? Made some money. Wasn't a fish sold in this city we didn't take a bite of. Climbed our way up the ladder, right? Makes this end-of-the-line deal more meaningful. Even with you about to shit your boxers as sorry-ass as can be, it's still more meaningful."

For the first time Lombardi didn't try to speak. He stared at Sal and shook his head sadly.

"Sal," Ben said. "The name."

"I don't need a name, you moron, so shut the fuck up!" Sal snarled the words over his shoulder then refocused on Lombardi. "This isn't about a name because we know the name, don't we, Lump? You and me both. Who doesn't in this town? Even hump-backed Mario in the butcher shop knows. Even retarded Tony Pooch at the Fish and Game Club. Any two-bit bagman on Mohawk Street knows the name, you stupid prick. How'd you think you'd get away with it? Do I look like Tony Pooch to you? Am I bald? Am I cross-eyed?"

Lombardi grunted a string of muffled, angry words, ending with what sounded like an attempt to spit. Spit? Ben thought. How could he spit through tape? There was no long *eeeeeeee* this time.

When Lombardi finished, Sal slapped his face hard five times, back and forth.

Lombardi's eyes shifted to Ben. "*Eeeeeeee*," he said, eyes pleading, his cheeks fire truck red. Then Lombardi began blubbering and rocking his great bulk back and forth like a lunatic in a straitjacket.

"Hey," Sal said to Ben. "He's speaking your language. He's sure not making sense to me."

"He's saying *please*," Ben said.

"No he's not," Sal said. "He's saying, *I'm a moron with fingers in the wrong cookie jar so I now I need to die before I shit myself.* Like that hack lawyer Brancusi. Like every stupid prick with his fat fingers in somebody else's jar." He turned to Ben. "OK, fun's over.

Go ahead. This is getting . . . stupid. Real stupid. So take care of it. Get it done."

Ben stared dumbly at Sal, then at Lombardi, still rocking crazily.

"Sal, you said scare him. You said we get the name and leave. That's what you said. That was the job."

Ben was awash with a feeling he remembered from high school, especially from math and English classes—that he was confused, lost, or slow; that he was out of a loop everyone else was in; that he was two steps behind even when charging ahead at full speed.

"What are you, stupid?" Sal said. "Why do you think you're here? You're not one of us, so you got to prove yourself. You got to prove who you are. Show me who the hell you are."

Sal backed against a wall so as not to get sprayed with blood. "Do it," he commanded. "Every goddamn second this jerk breathes is a waste of my time."

Ben's throat was so constricted he couldn't swallow. He closed his eyes, squeezed the trigger—and was surprised at the angry pop and kick.

"You dumb fuck!" Sal shouted. "You missed. You shot the fucking wall. Get up close. Do it right. He cocked his thumb and index finger like a handgun. Three in the head, *bam bam bam.* What's the matter with you? You're dumb as a mick."

Lombardi was now screaming as best he could while he rocked, sucking tape in and out.

"Do it!" Sal shouted.

Lombardi lurched to his feet, raising the chair on his back like a huge turtle shell. He hurled himself and the chair at Sal, whose head snapped against the brick wall then bounced forward. Sal's knees buckled, and he slumped to the floor, head flopped over and eyes shut. Lombardi tumbled over him in what seemed to Ben like eerie slow motion, wrists still taped together, the chair stuck on his back. Everything in the room seemed frozen. Then Lombardi twisted his head toward Ben and began grunting, furiously, like a stabbed pig.

"What's the name?" Ben asked Lombardi, pointing the gun at his head.

Lombardi stopped grunting and peered quizzically at Ben through narrowed, bloodshot eyes.

"What's the name?" Ben asked again. "That's the whole goddamn point, isn't it?"

Lombardi shook his head slowly and sadly. He moaned once, long and slow, sounding to Ben like a cow he'd heard once during a school trip to a farm.

Ben looked over at Sal, his head still flopped to one side, eyes still shut. Blood from a corner of his mouth ran a squiggly line to his chin.

Then Ben started shouting. "Tell me that fucking name you lowlife scumbag! I need that name right now! I can't spend my life pointing this gun at your crater-face while you grunt like a pig! I got a goddamn job to do!"

"*Eeeeeeee*," Lombardi screamed, vigorously nodding. "*Eeeeeeee.*"

Ben raised his face to the light bulb hanging from the ceiling. "Tell me!" he shouted. "For once in your life just tell me. Tell me what I need to know, or I'll blow your brains out!"

He fired three shots into the light. Sparks blasted out, and the room went dark. A smell of something burning filled the room.

"You deserved it, you bastard," Ben shouted at the ceiling. Now he was close to tears. "You lousy, stinking, nobody bastard, you always deserved it, because you never told me anything. Not never, and not once."

Home

"SO WHAT?" Vince said. "So he forgot to wipe his mouth. Who cares?"

At eight fifteen in the morning, Vince DeCarlo sat in his office, a windowless cleaning-supplies room with two chairs on a gray shag rug, a battered file cabinet, and a wooden desk with pink invoices strewn around a framed photograph of his wife. Set into the bottom corner of the frame was a snapshot of a smiling boy. A variety of boxes had been piled along the walls to the ceiling. Vince was drinking black coffee he'd poured from a thermos, talking with Doug Sessa, the youngest custodian on his staff.

"I'm telling you it was toothpaste. Fresh toothpaste."

"You can tell fresh from old?"

"Old toothpaste is dry."

"There's no law against brushing your teeth at work."

Doug shook his head and ran a hand lightly over his crew cut. "I'm saying the toothpaste explains what I heard during the late shift. I thought it was the heating system, but the furnace was fine. So I tracked it to the south storage room, which was locked. That's where Griff keeps spare parts, right? Then the noise stopped, everything dead quiet. But I'm telling you, when I saw Griff this morning, I knew what that noise was."

"What?"

"Snoring."

"That's bullshit."

"If it's bullshit, there's no harm checking out the storage room. Let's settle this right now."

"That's Griff's room—I leave parts and supplies to him. He can fix any broke thing in this school, and you know it. He worked construction for Tibald on the north side before they went bust. He's been here for ten years. With Griff, there's no surprises. He clocks in early. He never calls in sick. He brings that banged-up lunch box to work every day. At noon he eats a ham-and-cheese sandwich and drinks tea with milk and sugar from a Sears thermos exactly like the one I use. His wife puts a couple of these raisin cookie things in his lunch box—sweetest woman you'd ever meet. After Angela passed away, they invited me to dinner up in Remsen, and I ate ten of those damn cookies. Could have eaten ten more except it's rude. Griff's always clean shaved. He doesn't smell. See what I'm saying? There's no way his wife kicked him out. There's no way he's sleeping in a storage room."

"Come on, Vince. You got the master key. If I'm wrong, there's no harm. If I'm wrong, I buy you a six-pack."

"I don't drink, do I?"

"OK. Soda. I'll buy you a soda six-pack."

Vince stood out of his chair slowly, fingering the ring of keys attached to his belt. "Where's Griff now?"

"Working on the gym bleachers. Afterwards, he's got no reason to go to that storage room. Unless"—and here Doug smiled for the first time—"unless he left something at home."

VINCE PUSHED OPEN THE DOOR and flicked a switch that lit a bulb in the ceiling. He scanned the hallway. Cardboard boxes were stacked floor to ceiling on shelves that spanned the length of the hall.

"Jesus," he said. "Griff built-in these shelves. And labeled and alphabetized everything: ball bearings, bathroom tiles, brackets."

"Did you tell him to?"

"No, but it's a great idea. It's why he gets things done. He doesn't need me looking over his shoulder. Not like you," Vince added, "with that dumpster episode."

"You had to bring that up didn't you? I said I was sorry. And that was, like, six months ago."

"We don't run a public dump. You can't fill our dumpster with other people's crap. Especially toxic crap. What's that about anyway? You running a business on the side?"

"I said I was sorry. It was a one-time thing."

Vince pulled a large box labeled "Nuts and Bolts" off the shelf. Inside, he found smaller boxes, organized according to size. He turned to Doug. "This here's the best-organized supply room I ever saw. See why I leave Griff to himself?"

Doug squeezed past Vince to continue down the hall, occasionally setting a hand on a labeled box. He stopped at a black curtain on his left, hung from a rod attached to the ceiling.

"The hall's got an L shape," Doug said. "Did you know that?" He yanked the curtain open and flicked a switch on the wall. "Jesus Christ," he said. "Jesus H. Christ."

Six recessed track lights lit up, revealing fitted beige carpeting and walls painted off-white. In the far corner was a half-size refrigerator with an electric frying pan on top; pots and pans hung from a rack bolted to the ceiling. Floor-to-ceiling bookshelves crammed with paperbacks were fitted against the right-hand wall. A couch and a small round table with a reading lamp stood against the left wall, facing a TV with a rabbit-ear antenna on a chest of drawers. A photograph of Griff and his wife hung above the couch.

"Here's where he sleeps." Doug pointed to a loft with a retractable ladder. "Didn't I tell you? Didn't I say he was a freak? He's built a bedroom in a city high school. It doesn't take a brain surgeon to know what's on that guy's mind."

Vince pulled away a room divider near the couch. "Toilet," he said. He flicked a switch for a ceiling fan. "And a bathtub. How'd he get a bathtub in here? And plumbing? How'd he do that?"

"There's a girl's bathroom on the other side," Doug said. "He figured it all out. Better check for peepholes."

"You're talking about yourself," Vince said, "not Griff."

On a shelf over the bathtub, a hairbrush, toothbrush, and toothpaste tube were lined up, an inch apart. Vince started laughing. Doug hesitated, then laughed with him.

"Do you believe this guy?" Vince said. "Everything's crammed but nothing's crowded. And the workmanship." Vince ran a finger along the edge of the bookcase. "Custom-built, as plumb as can be."

"Vince." Doug lifted a framed document from the wall. "What's this? It's a bunch of gibberish."

"It's gotta be Welsh," Vince said, looking it over. "That's what he talks with his wife. And her name's at the top—Elizabeth: 1901–1964. Vince put a hand on his forehead. "Hey, it's a funeral program. She's dead. His wife is dead. She died this year."

"And then he moved into our storage room," Doug said. "That's what happened. Unbelievable. The guy says to himself, 'Now I'm gonna start living in a storage room in a city high school.'"

Vince was again scanning the room. "He carted in lumber and worked for how long? A month? Three months? Nobody knew. The guy . . ." He turned to Doug. "The guy's a genius."

"Must have been at it weekends and nights," Doug said. "So nobody heard. Sneaky, you know?"

"Ten dollars we find cheese and ham in the fridge," Vince said. "And milk. I'll be goddamned."

"Griff's senior guy on staff. What're you gonna do?"

"There's no choice." Vince shook his head. "I have to let him go."

"Remember that raccoon last winter?" Doug said. "It's like that. Nasty. Stunk everything up."

"Yeah, and it was your job to get rid of it."

"I wanted to," Doug said. "I brought my hunting rifle, remember?"

"You don't bring a gun to a school, you idiot. How can you not know that? It was Griff took care of it. Trapped it live and drove the thing to that country club. Which was it? Valley View, over by the zoo. And didn't make a big deal of it, did he? Now the raccoon lives in a golf course by the biggest dumpster in the city."

"Probably rabid," Doug said.

"Anyway," Vince said, "Griff did a beautiful job, didn't he? Better than my own goddamn place."

JUST BEFORE NOON Vince found Griff in the gym, setting tools into a battered metal toolbox.

"Will the bleacher railings hold?" Vince asked.

"I bolted them down good," Griff said. "They'll hold. And I had a word with Coach Henning. You wouldn't believe the state of his office. Shelves, a closet, a built-in desk would change everything. The guy might finally relax a little." Griff pulled a folded paper from his back pocket. "So I drew up a plan."

"Griff," Vince said. "We gotta talk."

"Just listen," Griff said. "I can fit in a cedar closet for uniforms. Moth resistant. And no more piles of junk, though they'll need to fold the uniforms. I can draw up a plan. What d'you think?"

"Here's what I think," Vince said. "We get some lunch. Does your wife still pack those cookies in your lunch box? The ones with raisins?"

"Currants," Griff said, looking away. "*Pice ar y maen*. Welsh cakes. And no, she doesn't. Just sandwiches now."

"I liked those cookies," Vince said.

"I know," Griff said. "Me too."

INSTEAD OF JOINING GRIFF FOR LUNCH, Vince went to his office and shut the door. He sat in his squeaky swivel chair. He stared around—at the dusty metal file cabinet, the bare walls, the brown shag rug that covered half the gritty concrete floor. "What the hell," he said. He took a sandwich from his lunch box and tossed it on the desk. "Who the hell cares?"

A knock on his door was followed by a quick, "You here?" Doug stepped in and closed the door. "What did you tell him?"

"Who?"

"Griff. You talked to him, right?"

"We talked."

"What'd you say? About him living like a raccoon."

Vince shook his head. "He's not living like a raccoon. He's living like a messed-up person."

"You didn't say anything?" Doug took a step closer. "I don't believe this. You're letting him stay, aren't you? In a goddamn storage room. In a school where girls walk through the front doors every day. Teenage girls who use bathrooms. You think no one notices the girls here?"

"You notice," Vince said. "But who cares where he lives? Who really cares? We all get out of bed in the morning, don't we? We go to work. We go home. For me it's a Genesee Street apartment in a building where I don't know anyone. You go some other place. Out

in Deerfield, right? You've got a toilet, a TV, a bed. He's got those.
Except somewhere along the line his home got messed up. Not the
way mine got messed up, but you know, ballpark. Or maybe he ran
out of money. If a wife gets sick and dies, that's expensive. I know
all about that. If a son grows up and wants nothing to do with you,
that's how it is, and your home just got smaller. And you want to
know something else? Those girls are safer with him living here."

"I can't believe this," Doug said. "This is fucked up."

"He's sixty-seven for Christ's sake. What's he going to do?
Where's he gonna go?"

"This isn't right," Doug said. "You think the principal wants a
creepy Welsh guy taking a bath in a storage room? Using a port-o-
potty for God's sake? You think that's gonna work? Why don't you
ask that prick history teacher his opinion—Johnson or Jackson or
Dickson. You think he'll think it's funny?"

"Griff's not creepy. He's messed up." Vince took a bite of his
sandwich and chewed. "I'm the same. A messed-up old guy. If I
hadn't stopped drinking, I'd be a dead old guy. I retire in two years.
Maybe I'll leave the Algonquin and move in with Griff. Be cheaper
too. Think he can make bunk beds?"

"Go ahead," Doug said. "Make a joke. That's your call. Be a
funny guy. Do whatever you want. But remember what I said." He
pointed a finger at Vince's face. "This isn't right. And someone's
gonna find out. And then you can only blame yourself."

"How about you?" Vince said. "You're in on this. What're you
going to do?"

"Me?" Doug opened the door. "I'm young, and I know the way
things are supposed to be. I'm not messed up. I'm not an old guy.
And I'm not losing this job."

Puzzle

KATE WAS WRITING AN ESSAY at her desk when her mother opened the door without knocking.

"What's the meaning of this, young lady?" she demanded, waving a creased letter.

Kate dropped her pen. Her eyes darted to her bed. With a painful wrench in her stomach she saw that the sheets and pillowcases had been changed.

"*I'm* supposed to strip the bed," Kate said, her voice strained and high-pitched. "That's *my* job."

"You didn't do your job, did you, though it's washing day. No, you were out riding your bike with friends having a grand time. And now I have to find this, and read this."

"You didn't have to."

"Of course I had to. Why wouldn't I?"

Kate leapt from her chair to snatch the letter, but her mother held it beyond her reach, saying, "I want to know what it means."

"It doesn't mean anything," Kate said miserably.

"A love letter," her mother said. She brought it to her nose and winced. "And stinking of perfume. And to your cousin Tom of all people. How many have you sent?"

"I never sent any. He doesn't know."

"Well," her mother said, "at least there's that. Why was it in your pillowcase?"

"I only wrote it yesterday."

"You slept with it. Daft girl. Sleeping with a letter. When were you planning on giving it to him?"

"I wasn't."

"I don't believe you," Kate's mother said. "Things have a purpose don't they? The purpose of a letter is to tell someone something. You hid this in your pillowcase until you could give it to him so he'd know what a silly girl you are."

"I wouldn't give it to him." Kate began crying, wiping away tears with her fingers. "I couldn't bear to."

"Then why did you write the thing?"

"I had to."

"You didn't have to," her mother said. "This isn't homework. No one forced you."

"I kept thinking. Thinking and thinking. I hoped writing would make the thinking stop."

"And did it?"

Kate moved to sit on the edge of her bed. She scratched a rash on her arm. "It felt good to write the letter," she said in a quiet voice. "But I haven't stopped thinking."

"And you put it in your pillowcase so you'd feel close to him while you slept? So you might dream about this boy. Is that it? Is that what it comes to?" She shook her head. "Stupid, stupid girl."

Kate's mother slipped the letter into a pocket of her apron. "I'll destroy this," she said. "I'll burn it, and we will forget it ever existed. Do you understand me? Your father would be furious if he knew. And his own nephew, three years your senior. Your father wouldn't let you out of his sight."

"It only says my feelings," Kate said.

"Your feelings? Your feelings are the rungs of a ladder from which you will fall and never rise up again."

"Will you tell Dad?" Kate asked. "He hates me enough already."

"He doesn't hate you. He just doesn't understand."

"Why does he say those embarrassing things about me in front of people, even in front of Tom?"

"It's his way. He doesn't know another way."

"So will you tell him?"

Her mother let a few seconds pass.

"There are some things—many things—he doesn't need to know. But you must understand that in this house nothing is kept from me. A mother knows everything. That's because we do everything. We feel everything. You'll keep secrets from your father and your brother, but not from me."

"You never wrote a letter to a boy?" Kate asked, then bit her lip, wondering if the question would provoke another round of abuse.

"Of course not," her mother said. "And I'm surprised you'd ask such a thing. But we live in different times, don't we? You and I are from different worlds."

She stared hard at her daughter, her pinched expression softening.

"You believe that I'm strict. That I'm a difficult mother. That I won't let you do what you need to do. But you didn't know your Nain, and maybe that's a blessing."

"Why a blessing?"

"Stop that!" Her mother pointed to where Kate was scratching her arm. "It'll get infected."

Kate dropped her hand to her side.

"All right," her mother said. "I'll tell you a story about your Nain. Maybe it'll help you understand. Maybe you'll see how easy things are for you. And how different they were for me." She sat next to her daughter on the bed.

"How do I begin?" She closed her eyes. When she opened them, she'd made a decision. "When I was your age," she said, "living in Wales, a boy asked if I'd walk with him up Bryn Heulog. 'There's a good view,' he told me, which of course I knew perfectly well. Didn't we both live in the same village? Hadn't I walked up and down that hill many times? The minister had called a meeting of the congregation for that afternoon—my parents and brothers were going, and I was to stay home and wash the dinner dishes. But I wanted to walk up Bryn Heulog with that boy. He asked me to meet him at two o'clock. It's all I could think of wanting."

"And did you?" Kate asked.

"I washed and dried the dishes, pots and pans, put everything in the cupboards quick as I could, then ran to meet him behind the post office where the footpath begins. I'd never done washing up that fast in my life. You see, I was as daft as you, though I had the sense never to write letters. But the boy wasn't where he said he'd be. I had to wait, with no way of telling the time. I was terribly nervous standing there, peeking round to the street, wondering what was keeping him, terrified someone would see me. I still remember how my heart pounded—I was sure he had forgotten. And for me, the girl I was then—that would be the end of the world."

"Or was it a trick?" Kate asked. "And he never meant to come?"

"No," her mother snapped. "Of course it wasn't a trick. He wasn't that sort of boy. He was kind and good."

"Was Dad the boy?"

"No."

"What was his name?"

"The name doesn't matter."

"And did he come at last?"

"He didn't," Kate's mother said. "My mother arrived in her chapel best, walking directly to where I was hiding. She carried the cane Sunday school teachers used to keep discipline. And she beat me with that, on my head, my face, my shoulders, my back. I wanted to run but knew that running would earn a worse beating later, at home, because where was I to go? Who in that village would protect me? I stood where I was until she tired of beating me, then followed her down the road. I followed but didn't make a sound and didn't shed a tear."

"How did she know?" Kate asked. "Did the boy tell?"

"No, he'd never betray me. I never knew how she found out. And that's the point of the story. Mothers always know. We can't help knowing. We can't help feeling. Even when we don't want to know or feel, we do. And we pass that on to our daughters, as I am doing now, with you."

"Did you talk with that boy after?"

"I did not."

"But you must have seen him again, around the village."

"I saw him. But we didn't talk. What would be the point?"

"Do you think Nain ever wanted to meet a boy, and her mother stopped her and beat her with a stick?"

"Enough," Kate's mother said wearily. She looked closely at her daughter, then leaned to kiss her forehead. "We've said more than enough. Finish your homework, and we'll put this foolishness behind us."

"You're taking my letter? Please let me keep it. I would never send it. I just want to have it."

"Of course I'm taking that letter. I'm destroying it as I said I would. That way, no one else will ever know. It's as if it never happened. Just a story you'll someday tell your own daughter."

AFTER HER MOTHER LEFT, KATE shut the door, threw herself on her bed, and cried long and hard, covering her face with a pillow so she wouldn't be heard.

When she had exhausted herself from crying, she slowly rose, sat on the bed, wiped her face and swollen eyes with her fingers, and stood. She opened the door and peered down the empty hall, then shut the door. She opened her closet door and knelt on the hardwood floor in front of a stack of boxed puzzles, stored there since she was a child. A dozen boxes, including a complicated jigsaw with a thousand pieces—a present for her last birthday that she'd never opened. Each birthday she'd be given a new, more complex puzzle to demonstrate, her mother explained, how quickly she was growing up. But she'd become bored with puzzles long ago, and it was more and more difficult to pretend to be grateful for the annual birthday present. She pulled out and opened the box at the bottom of the stack. Instead of the original wooden pieces—large squares, rectangles and triangles for a three-year-old—the box was filled with pink envelopes. With both hands, Kate moved the envelopes around in the box, sliding one over another, mixing them up. She lifted one out, held it to her nose, inhaling. Lavender. She removed a page from the envelope, unfolded it, and read it. Then reread it. She brought the page to her lips, closed her eyes, kissed it, refolded it, and slid it back into the envelope and the envelope back into the box, which she returned to the bottom of the stack.

When she settled at her desk to finish her essay, Kate felt better. She didn't worry about what her mother knew or didn't know or thought she knew. Kate felt better than she had the entire day.

Naked

RUTH COULDN'T IMAGINE how she'd get through the day. She was five months pregnant—and far more tired and anxious than she remembered being when she was carrying Brynley.

She'd been up at dawn to cook breakfast and pack a lunch for Robert, who had to be on the construction site downtown by six thirty and wouldn't be home until seven that evening. Brynley hadn't settled to sleep—no matter how she rocked him, walked him, sung to him, he'd woken up and cried every hour until, at four in the morning, she'd finally brought him to their bed. "The invasion of the body snatcher," Robert called it, since their fourteen month old insisted on sleeping between them. Why wouldn't Brynley sleep? Why must he be so busy, jamming into his mouth anything not nailed down? Especially anything small enough to choke him. They'd converted a bedroom into a playroom, where she'd taped over every electric socket and moved anything breakable out of reach. Thank God there was a door to shut, so he couldn't crawl down the hall into the kitchen or to the dimly lit staircase leading to the laundry room they shared with Mrs. Edwards in the ground-floor apartment. And yet, with all the safety precautions, there wasn't a day in which Brynley didn't cry out because of a fresh cut or scrape—often she couldn't tell how it happened, in a room devoid of edges. But of course she'd hug him, comfort him, and apply the bandages.

Brynley wouldn't tolerate the playpen they'd bought a year ago—and the thing wasn't cheap. As soon as he was in it, encircled by his favorite stuffed animals, his mother leaning over and smiling, he'd start screaming, rattling the bars like an angry monkey in a cage until she lifted him out. So Ruth gave the playpen to her friend Charlene, whose daughter Theresa—a sweet child with blond curls framing a very round face—took to it immediately. She'd *ask* to be put in and cry when lifted out.

Ruth planned to devote this morning to grocery shopping. It wouldn't be easy getting on and off the bus with Brynley, the stroller, and the grocery bags, but there was no choice—she was out of milk and vegetables. She also needed to visit Mrs. Edwards, who'd gone into Faxton Hospital three weeks earlier. Though she liked her downstairs neighbor, Ruth dreaded those visits, especially the sour smell of the cancer ward. Brynley, strangely, didn't mind—he smiled and laughed and made faces at Mrs. Edwards, propped on pillows on the hospital bed. The only respite might be at three o'clock, when she'd offered to babysit Charlene's daughter—there was a chance that the two children would amuse each other.

RUTH MADE TEA and sliced and buttered bread while Charlene encouraged the children to play together. But Brynley was too involved with pulling a marble eye out of his favorite Teddy bear to notice Theresa, who craned her neck left and right—looking everywhere except at Brynley, now crawling to the opposite wall to collapse a tower of blocks. Ruth enjoyed her talks with Charlene, who liked to gossip about the women in the Bethesda choir: how Catherine Tudor was furious that she hadn't been a soloist all year, how Jones the choir director couldn't keep his eyes off Jane Evans, who'd been gaining weight around her middle. Ruth didn't like nasty gossip, the kind that ruins marriages and friendships. But she felt that Charlene kept her in touch with the outer world while her own world was every minute taken up with Robert, Brynley, the kitchen, the apartment, and the baby to come.

When Charlene left for her doctor's appointment, Theresa was busy stacking blocks into a new tower, perilously crooked. Meanwhile, Brynley had moved on to his car set, crashing one into another repeatedly. At least they weren't squabbling or crying. But she thought it odd that the children kept so separate, as if the other were invisible, or a creature of no consequence. She brought her cup of tea to a window facing the cheerless back yard: pocked driveway, her neighbor's lopsided garage, a tree in the midst of unmowed grass, its thick roots bowed up into the air, the branches weighed down with apples. This was her world, more than a little run down, narrow and circumscribed, but safe at least—as safe as she could make it. What she knew of the goings-on in the greater world, from the TV or radio, frightened her: the war in Vietnam, a civil rights march in Washington, a robbery and murder in a bar on James Street.

Ruth sat on the small couch, setting her cup and saucer on the coffee table. Theresa was pulling a dress over the head of her naked doll. Brynley was still crashing cars, shouting "Bam! Bam!" Ruth kicked off her shoes and locked her hands over her belly. How did she get so big so fast? She didn't remember ever feeling this huge with Brynley. She tried to relax in the way the doctor had instructed, breathing slowly and steadily, in and out, with eyes shut. She imagined the baby also relaxing, suspended, like her, for a moment in time. She and Robert hadn't planned on another so soon—maybe after three or four more years, when they'd have more saved up. When they started sleeping together after Brynley's birth, they were careful—but not careful enough.

RUTH OPENED A DOOR that led from her bedroom into a meadow. Robert was with her, and Brynley, too, walking unsteadily but refusing to hold her hand. When had he started walking? It was true what everyone told her about children growing up so fast. Further down the meadow, Mrs. Edwards was standing with her hands on her narrow hips, smiling, wearing the dress that she often wore to Bethesda services. Brynley took off running toward Mrs. Edwards with astonishing confidence and speed, and the old lady snatched him up and held his face close to her own. But Ruth wasn't worried about Mrs. Edwards dropping her boy. *He's safe*, she thought, for no good reason. *He's perfectly safe.*

Her next thought was, *My tea!* She opened her eyes and zeroed in on the floral-patterned china cup and saucer, intact on the coffee table. "Brynley!" she called out. "Theresa!" She saw that the door was open wide enough for an infant to crawl through. How on earth? "Brynley!" she shouted again, lumbering to her feet. The baby chose that moment to kick so violently that Ruth collapsed back onto the couch, stunned by the pain. She allowed herself one deep breath before standing and moving, as quickly as she could, to the kitchen, her hands under her belly.

"Brynley, come here this instant!" she called, desperate. She saw a sneaker on the linoleum floor. Had she left out a knife? She had—a bread knife on the counter—but neither he nor Theresa were in the kitchen. She felt dizzy as the next terror gripped her. The stairs to the laundry room! She tossed the knife in the sink and made her way quickly down the hall where, sure enough, she saw another open door. "No!" she screamed. The previous Saturday she herself had nearly tumbled down those stairs with an over-full wicker basket of clothes.

She peered at the bottom landing, making out an indistinct heap in the shadow beyond the last step. She gripped the railing—which felt flimsy under her full weight—and worked her way down the uncarpeted stairs, heart pounding. The heap was Brynley's T-shirt, his other sneaker, Theresa's sandals, two white socks. A few feet further on—the doll, stripped of clothes, face down.

They weren't in the laundry room, but the door to the backyard was open—and Ruth saw two diapers and Theresa's smock on the stoop. Beyond and to the left, her neighbor's garage—with red paint peeling off in long strips—seemed about to collapse inward.

And then she saw them.

They were naked on the grass under the tree, legs smeared with dirt, in the midst of fallen apples. Brynley was touching Theresa's head, lifting and dropping her blond curls, intent and serious while Theresa hiccupped with laughter. Then Theresa ran her fingers over Brynley's face, nose, mouth, eyes. She was focused and serious while he laughed the same laugh he'd give after a bout of nursing.

Ruth watched them taking turns, touching and laughing, laughing and touching.

Monkey's Uncle

RILEY'S WAS A LONG, DARK TAVERN on the corner of Auburn and Genesee—the oldest in the neighborhood. A scattering of men, alone or in pairs, drank whiskey and beer and spoke in low tones on stools along the wooden bar or in booths against the back wall. Many of these men could be seen in Riley's any time of day or night, from when J. C. Riley opened at ten in the morning until last call at midnight.

On a Tuesday afternoon, just after three o'clock, Old Llew looked up from the corner booth, where he was drinking his Utica Club and thumbing through the newspaper's sports section, to see the front door open, letting in a blast of sunlight and a man in his mid-twenties. The man's shape was familiar, thin and gangly, though it took Llew a minute to recognize Nye, his niece's son, in blue jeans and black T-shirt.

Nye walked to the bar warily, as if afraid someone might order him to leave. And indeed, Riley—in khaki trousers, pressed white shirt, green bow tie—looked askance at this new customer. With the exception of Old Llew, the other drinkers didn't turn their heads. Nye examined a large, cloudy mason jar of pickled eggs displayed on the bar, the only food in sight. He set a finger on the glass, opposite a grayish egg, and drew an egg-size oval.

"Those aren't for sale," J. C. told him. "This is a drinking establishment."

"Utica Club. Bottle," Nye said, not taking his eyes off the egg. "I don't eat mummified eggs."

"They're *pickled*," J. C. told him. "They're for show."

"Yes they are," Nye said. "Best in show, I'd say."

When Nye settled on a barstool, his left leg began vibrating, as if plugged into an electric socket. J. C. brought the bottle, and Nye had a long, greedy chug before taking out a wallet and laying five dollars on the bar, which J. C. picked up.

Llew shook his head. Hadn't Ceridwen told him Nye was finishing treatment at Marcy State? His memory of his last visit with his niece wasn't very clear.

J. C. returned with Nye's change, then busied himself replenishing bottles in the glass-fronted cooler, glancing occasionally in Nye's direction.

"Howza!"

All eyes shifted to Nye, who maintained his slouched posture, head bowed as if in prayer.

J. C. strode down the bar. "Is there something you need?"

"Same again," Nye said.

J. C. set the empty under the counter and removed a bottle from the cooler. After taking Nye's money he said, sharply, "If you want a drink in this tavern, you'll ask politely or you'll leave."

Silent, head still bowed low, Nye avoided eye contact.

J. C. retreated to the other end of the bar, keeping a line of vision to this unfamiliar customer. Llew knew the old man—a former bantamweight with a short temper—was planning how to dispatch poor Nye should the need arise. One uppercut to the chin would do it.

Llew folded his newspaper on the table and raised a thumb. J. C. —always attuned to his regulars—nodded. With a hand on the table and another on his cane, Llew levered himself from his booth. He limped to the bar, dropping heavily on the stool next to Nye.

"Duw Duw," he said, catching his breath. "I hiked a fair mile just then."

Nye glanced at Llew, and raised his bottle for a chug.

"How have you been?" Llew asked.

"I don't speak with strangers," Nye said. He wiped his mouth with his sleeve. "Unless he buys me a beer. Then we might have words."

"I'm your Uncle Llew. You've always known me."

Nye's left cheek twitched. A spasm squeezed his eyes shut. He opened them slowly. "You're not," he said.

"Then who am I?"

"An imposter."

J. C. appeared, wiping the bar in front of Llew with a rag then setting the glass of beer where he'd wiped. "All right, Mr. Powell?" he said. "Any concerns? I'm more than glad to help."

"I'm fine, thank you, Mr. Riley," Llew said. "No concerns. And how are you?"

J. C. glanced at Nye before answering. "As good as can be among the wasters and the touched."

"Mr. Riley, this is my niece's son, Nye Harris."

J. C.'s eyes widened. "Is that so?"

"It is. Nye, shake the man's hand. Mr. Riley is our landlord, therefore lord of this establishment. Those who don't mind Mr. Riley regret it soon enough."

When Nye put out his hand, Llew saw the fingers tremble.

"Good to meet you," Nye said, still avoiding eye contact.

J. C. shook the hand and retreated down the bar.

"So," Llew said, "how are you?"

"I'm incredible," Nye said. He snorted. "I'm unexplainable."

"And what brings you here?"

"Thirst." Nye was staring straight ahead. "Been thirsty my whole life. Can't quench it."

"Nye," Llew said. "You don't want to travel my road. That's not for you. It's not really for me either."

"You're hogging the road," Nye said. "It's the road not taken. Except it is."

"As for me," Llew said, "I'm here for the ambience."

"As for you," Nye said, "you're Uncle Stranger, aren't you? Stranger than truth."

"I'm your great uncle," Llew said. "You recognize me, don't you? It hasn't been that long."

"You have his face," Nye said, still refusing to look at Llew. "Where'd you find it?"

"It's been mine a good while. And more's the pity. So, you're out of hospital?"

"I'm cured, aren't I?" Nye said. "I'm a thousand percent, aren't I?"

"Are you? That's wonderful. How'd that happen?"

"I don't remember."

"You don't?"

"I don't."

"Surely," Llew said, "you remember something."

"They took me to a room with a chair. They anointed my head with light. They said I was cured. Like a slab of bacon. Like an egg in a jar. And they didn't lie for once. But it wasn't them that cured me. It was God, because God doesn't lie. God cured me with light. And God forgives memories."

"Are you at the group home?" Llew asked. "Or with your mother?"

Nye jerked his head toward the door. "With your mother. But I'm not with her now."

"Does she know you're here?"

"Does she know *you're* here?" Nye raised his bottle, drained it, set it on the bar by the jar of pickled eggs.

Llew sipped his draft. "What's next, now you're cured?"

"Howza!" Nye shouted.

J. C. rushed over. "You make that ungodly rumpus again," he said, jabbing a finger at Nye's face, "and you're out. I don't care whose people you are. You're out on your arse."

"All right, Mr. Riley," Llew said. "My great-nephew would like a beer. I believe that's what he's communicating. Correct, Nye? To quench his thirst. And he'll behave, I promise. I'll take—I'll take full responsibility."

J. C. gave Nye a sidelong glance before setting another bottle in front of him.

"He's a dog," Nye said when J. C. had left.

"Pardon?"

"He's a dog that's been kicked. That's why he bites. Old dogs can't learn new tricks, but they remember old kicks."

"Ah now, we won't speak of Mr. Riley in that manner," Llew said. "He's a grumpy old dog is all."

"Cerberus," Nye said. "With a bow tie and teeth."

"Yes," Llew allowed. "A few teeth."

"I'm going to the Adirondacks," Nye said before taking a pull on his beer. "I want to be alone."

"Alone?"

"More alone. I want to live in a cabin, alone. In the woods, alone. No medicine. No white light. No God who loves me, his wonders to perform. No secret room with a wasp buzzing, stinging my brain. No mother, wondering. Alive, alone in a woods-alone-cabin with my honeybees in my bee-loud glade." He glanced slyly at Llew. "No Uncle Stranger either, no sir. No Uncle Stranger who shows up when he likes, for a good meal." He took another long pull on his bottle. "No questions. No answers."

"I do have one question," Llew said. "Have you been taking your medicine?"

"Electricity is the fingernail of God, and it scratched my forehead. So I'm cured. No medicine required. I'm as cured as you."

Old Llew sipped his beer, thinking it time to return to his table and newspaper. He'd tried his best. If anyone asked, he'd tried to talk sense to the boy. Now he could, in good conscience, go home to his corner booth and newspaper.

"You like to drink," Nye said. "Uncle Statue is who you are. Uncle Wounded and Uncle Stranger. And you like to drink."

"You noticed," Llew said. "You're like me, standing back and noticing. A statue I suppose. And I like to drink. That's true."

"They talk about you, Uncle Stranger. When you're not there, they talk."

"Who?"

"The talkers. Even the ones who don't."

"I'm never there, and I deserve every word they say," Llew said. "And more."

"No," Nye said. "That's not true."

"Why not?"

"Because you're an imposter."

"I'm not an imposter. I'm Llew Wynne Powell, your mother's uncle. I told you that, and I wish you'd remember. When you were a boy, I'd bring you to the zoo on Saturday afternoons."

"My monkey's uncle," Nye said. "You're my monkey's uncle, with wonders to perform."

"Yes, well, there's no point arguing, is there? Either I am your Uncle Llew or I'm not."

"You're not who they say you are."

Old Llew set a hand on the bar to steady himself.

"What do you mean? Who do they say I am?"

"A hopeless case. But you're not," Nye said. "You're an imposter. It's not the same, no matter what they say around the dinner table. You're not the town-bloody-drunk-nobody. You don't stink like you pissed yourself. You're not buggered, cockeyed, cooked."

"Cooked?" Llew said. "Buggered?" He laughed—he couldn't help himself. "Enough. Enough about what I am or am not."

"You don't sweat beer. You don't mess the bathroom floor."

"But I do!" Llew protested. "In fact I do!"

"You're not fried, hootered, blootered, lacquered, polluted, loused, legless, pissed as a parrot."

"Bloody hell," Llew said, laughing. "Do they really say those things?"

"You're not pickled tanked blinded bladdered three-sheets-to-the-winded paralyticed shnockered slaughtered stewed Schlitzed toasted or twatted."

"Stop, would you for God's sake?" Llew's eyes teared up. "Twatted? They wouldn't say that."

"I'm an imposter, too," Nye said. "Nephew Stranger. Son Stranger. It's *my* wonder to perform." He drained his bottle. "An imposter," he added, "imposing, like you. A pickled egg. My monkey's nephew."

"Yes, you are," Llew said, and clinked Nye's bottle with his glass. "Whatever you say you are, you are, even more than you were. Before today I hardly knew you could talk, let alone spout poetry."

"How-*za-za-za-ZA*!" Nye barked, squeezing his eyes shut. He slammed his bottle down on the bar.

"That's it," J. C. bellowed. "Fuck off, the both of you. They'll be no carrying on in my tavern. Get the hell out."

"We were just leaving, Mr. Riley," Old Llew said, producing his wallet and tossing a few dollars on the bar.

"You haven't finished." Nye pointed to Llew's half-full glass.

"We're well finished. Come along. Cerberus must keep his bite to himself this afternoon."

OUT ON THE SIDEWALK Llew and Nye stared around. *Goldfinger* was playing at the Uptown Theater across Genesee Street. It was a bright September midafternoon, and sunlight made Llew uncomfortable. Cars passed by steadily, heading downtown. A boy walked out of King Cole's, licking vanilla ice cream in a cone. Down the road, a pick-up truck pulled into the White Tower parking lot. Llew tapped his cane on the sidewalk. Then he slid his arm through his nephew's. "Will you take me home?" he said. "I'm twatted."

"Where's home?"

Llew thought about this. "Usually Riley's corner booth of an afternoon. But what about your mother's for now? She must be worried."

"That house is full of questions."

"We should go there," Llew said. "I can walk it, I think, though it's a journey. Will you attend me? I haven't seen Ceridwen in a while. I wasn't at my best the last visit . . ."

"Whoever sees her?" said Nye. "She's the monkey's mother."

"She's not so bad," Llew said. "She keeps a tidy house."

They walked arm in arm, following Genesee Street towards downtown, crossing Burrstone Road and Memorial Parkway, turning right onto Pleasant Street. They paused across from Baron von Steuben on his pedestal, brooding in his long, black cloak. They didn't talk but looked around at cars streaming by; at the willows, maples, and oaks fully leafed on the median; at the well-kept houses along Pleasant, some with flowers bordering their front sidewalks— pansies, bloodroot, daffodils. "The desert in bloom," Llew said, approvingly. They walked another few blocks, but at the corner of Pleasant and Oneida, Llew sat on a bus stop bench. Nye stood at his side.

"I've forgotten what it's like to sit under a sky and not be afraid," Llew said. "For some reason, the sun doesn't burn the eyes today. It only warms them. Can we wait until I get my breath?"

"I've got time," Nye said.

"Look at that one," Llew said, pointing his cane at General Casimir Pulaski on a pedestal in the median. "The archangel drawing his sword, defending grass from those who trample. And across the road—the park, South Woods, the ski slope. And further down the Parkway—the golf course, where none of us has walked. And the zoo at the crest of the hill. Do you remember, Nye? You cried for the monkeys huddled in their dark cages, so I bought you popcorn and you fed the pigeons. You asked if monkeys could cry. You were young, but I remember. And beyond the zoo, the cemetery with its gravestones overlooking all of us. Your little brother Billy is buried there. And your father. It's been a long time. I'd truly forgotten. I'm sorry, but truly I had forgotten."

Two teenage boys in sweatshirts and blue jeans, smoking cigarettes, approached them. The shorter one stopped and turned to stare at Nye and Llew. His friend also stopped. "Jesus," the short boy said to Llew, "you're an old bag of bones ain't you? Just a messy old bag of bones."

"Yes, an old bag," Llew said, without looking at the boy. "That's correct."

"Old bag," Nye said, "or young bag. No matter. We all empty out. Like Dad and Billy. Just look beyond the zoo."

The boy fixed his attention on Nye. "What's that? What're you saying? You looking for trouble?"

"No trouble," Llew said. "A bag is a bag, is all. Troubling but not trouble, if you see the difference."

"Mental," the boy told his friend. "From Marcy State. Let's go. They're only taking up space."

WHEN LLEW HAD DIFFICULTY standing from the bench, Nye took hold of his hands to pull him to his feet, and they walked slowly arm-in-arm until they reached Steuben Street, leading into Corn Hill on their left. Ten minutes later, arms still linked, they stood before Nye's mother's front porch.

"We've arrived unannounced," Llew said. "Ceridwen won't like that. Should have given a trumpet blast." He touched the lowest porch step with his cane.

"Maybe," Nye said. He looked worried. "You'll come in? It's nearly supper. There'll be food soon."

"I have one condition," Llew said.

"What's that?"

"We pretend to be who we are, and no one else."

Nye snorted, and his snort progressed into louder snorts. It took a moment for Llew to realize that his nephew was laughing.

"And no one else!" Nye shouted.

His laughing got Llew laughing, and they stood there laughing until the front door opened to show Ceridwen in her tan house dress and red-and-white checked apron. She frowned at them, wiping her hands with a dishtowel. She flipped the towel over a shoulder and stepped onto the porch.

"What have we here?" she said.

"It's me," Nye told her, "and no one else."

"And no one else," Llew echoed.

"A pair of no ones you are, aren't you?" Ceridwen said. "My son and my uncle. My ball and my chain." She sighed heavily. "Nye, you didn't tell me you were going out. I've been worried. You're just home from hospital. Where have you been?"

"Walking," Nye told her. He looked up at the sky, and then to his left.

"Yes, we've come a long way," Llew said. "Further than I could imagine. I walked through the wilderness, waylaid by wild beasts. But an angel attended me."

"Is that so?"

"Wait a moment. Wait . . . The wilderness. How does it go? Help me Ceridwen. You know this. Through the wilderness, through a land of deserts and pits, through a land of . . . of thirst . . . and . . . and what else?"

"And the shadow of death," Ceridwen said. "Jeremiah."

"Yes," Llew said. "A prophet's words. I knew you'd remember. A chapel girl wouldn't forget. The shadow of death. Yet I fear the evil. A cloud can block the sun, can't it? Or a mountain. You know as well as me."

Ceridwen shook her head, producing a tight little smile. "All right then," she said. "You'd better come in for a cup of tea, you and your angel. Be careful on those steps—Nye will help you. You'll both explain yourselves, you'll talk some sense to me, and then you'll stay for supper.

Father

SIÂN HAD INTENDED ON STAYING AWAY until Thanksgiving, when she'd *have* to go home because the dorms would close. But here she was, a week before Halloween in her parents' living room, standing by the fire place with the Welsh china dogs staring at each other from opposite ends of the mantelpiece, making small talk with neighbors and friends, eating finger sandwiches at a reception organized by white-haired ladies from church whose names she didn't want to remember. Mrs. Hughes? Mrs. Watkins? Mrs. James? Mrs. Richards? They looked the same as when she knew them growing up, but smaller—not shrunken, just smaller. She'd sat through the surprisingly brief funeral for Auntie Em at Bethesda, but since her family was hosting the reception, she couldn't leave. She'd have to wait until noon the next day before her father would drive her to the train station so she could reenter the new life she'd begun two months earlier.

Everyone at the reception who knew Siân asked the same questions, as if they'd agreed beforehand on a list: *Do you like college? What's your major? Have you made friends?* And then, coyly, *Is there a boy in your life?* They'd ask the questions in the same order, narrowing from abstract to intimate, and she'd dutifully answer: *Yes, I like it, English major, I've made friends, there's no boy.* The last was true if spoken in the present tense. There is no boy. There *was* a boy, but there *is* no boy. And she'd smile, returning the coyness back to the questioner.

They'd met at the orientation dance. And during the six weeks when there was a boy, she'd gotten pregnant. She spent two weeks in a state of panic, confiding to no one, not the boy, not even her roommate. Then one night she felt ill, threw up in a bathroom stall down the hall from her room, and felt her insides cramp. The contractions were so painful she passed out. And when her roommate found her in the stall an hour later, she'd miscarried.

There was a boy in her life, and there wasn't. There was a baby, and there wasn't. And then . . . ? Siân said to herself. And then? That was the question no one would ask, the most important, the question she couldn't bear to contemplate. *What happens next?*

"Excuse me." A man in his early twenties in a dark suit and maroon tie had turned toward Siân. "Did you know her? The . . . woman who passed away?" He held a cucumber sandwich in front of his mouth.

"Aunt Em," Siân said. "I called her Aunt Em when I was little."

"I see," he said, nodding. "I see."

Of course, he didn't see anything. Aunt Em or Uncle Roger weren't blood relatives, but they were in the house or about to arrive or preparing to leave ever since Siân could remember. There were Mam and Dad, and in the living room or kitchen, opening a door or shutting it, washing dishes or watching television, were Em and Roger. They'd arrive for Sunday dinners, Monday night bridge, Christmas shopping excursions. Siân, her brother Edward, her parents, and Em and Roger vacationed together—a shared cottage on Cape Cod, twin cabins on Indian Lake in the Adirondacks. Aunt Em babysat Siân and Edward regularly—she was lively, pretty, fun to be around. She'd play games that their mother refused to play: charades, hide-and-seek, pin the tail on the donkey. "If I had children," she'd tell them, "I'd want a boy and a girl just like you."

But it all changed as Siân started high school. And the strange thing was, no one acknowledged the change. One Sunday Em and Roger didn't arrive for dinner. Siân's mom said that Roger wasn't feeling well. The following evening, dour old Mr. and Mrs. Thomas from church replaced Em and Roger at the bridge table. When they didn't show up for dinner the next Sunday, Siân walked into the kitchen to ask her mother why.

"They're just not coming," her mother said.

"But why?"

"They're busy tonight, dear."

"Doing what?"

"I'm not sure."

"But they're always here for Sunday dinner." Siân felt tears gathering, a panic she didn't understand stirring in her chest.

"Well," her mother said as she emptied a pot of steaming potatoes into a colander, "plans change don't they? You'll see them again soon."

But Siân didn't see them for a long while.

"Why aren't Aunt Em and Uncle Roger in church anymore?" she asked her dad soon after they'd stopped coming to Sunday dinners.

"They've been on vacation," he said. "North Carolina, I think."

"Without us?"

"I only get two weeks off," he said. "So it didn't work this time. And it's Roger's cousin they're visiting—a family thing."

It was soon normal for Sunday dinners to include only their family. The Thomases continued to fill out the bridge table on Monday nights. And when Aunt Em and Uncle Roger at last showed up in church, they were polite but removed, distant, and left as soon as the service finished.

Siân felt that now, having been away at college, she better understood something about how relationships change—how even friends you thought would be with you for a lifetime could slip away. Her best friend from kindergarten, Melissa Eldridge, had moved to New Jersey years ago, and while they phoned each other on Saturday nights, soon the expensive phone calls became letters, the letters became postcards, and those became . . . nothing. Silence. And Georgina, Siân's closest neighbor friend, began hanging out with a greaser crowd shortly after they both started high school. Now neither she nor Siân acknowledged they'd ever had a friendship, each embarrassed by their connection for different reasons.

"Well, I'm really sorry," the man with the cucumber sandwich said. Siân had forgotten he'd begun a conversation. He bit his sandwich and chewed thoughtfully. "Your Aunt Em was young."

"Yes," Siân said. "That's true."

"Was she married?"

"Yes," she said. "To Roger"—she no longer thought of him as *Uncle* Roger. Pale and tense, Roger had stayed at the reception barely a half-hour before heading out the door. He didn't seem to recognize Siân.

"What do *you* do?" the young man asked. "No, don't tell me. Let me guess." He looked her up and down. "You're in college, right?"

Siân foresaw the coming questions. She scanned the room, catching sight of her father carrying a stack of dishes to the kitchen.

"I'm so sorry," she said, "but I can't talk right now. It's my father. I promised to help him clear dishes."

"Of course," he said. "But find me later, OK? I'm here with my grandmother who knows everyone. I'd like to talk some more. About what you're doing in college. If you feel like it."

Siân glanced at his right hand—no ring.

"Maybe," she said. "I'll see."

WHEN SHE'D ARRIVED at the train platform at Union Station the previous evening, Siân had felt oddly nervous carrying her little suitcase towards her father, hugging him and, immediately, smelling him—that distinctive father smell that she'd forgotten, that was his and only his. When they pulled apart, tears filled her eyes.

"Yes," he said. "It's sad. A terrible shock. Em of all people. An aneurism apparently."

But Siân wasn't thinking about Aunt Emily. She was thinking about what had happened to her at college, how she wanted to give her dad a glimpse of what she'd lost. The boy. The baby she didn't want. There, and gone.

The ride home was punctuated with disengaged questions about her courses and professors, and Siân's mechanical answers.

"Why are *we* hosting the reception?" she suddenly asked when they pulled into the driveway. She hoped she didn't sound too callous. "You and Mom haven't been close to Em and Roger for years."

He nodded. "Your mother . . . your mother didn't want to host when Reverend Price asked. But I just couldn't . . . you know, couldn't not remember her."

SIÂN'S DAD had piled the dishes in the sink and gone somewhere else. To the bathroom? Upstairs? She gazed around the kitchen. God, she could use a drink. If this were an Irish wake, she thought—like the one for Pat Noonan, who worked with her dad for years—there'd be whiskey, beer, and wine, with half empty glasses on every table. That family was raucous, telling stories and laughing. "Uncle Pat would want us to have fun," Mr. Noonan's nephew Danny had told her. "If he could, he'd be drinking and singing and telling stories with us."

Siân was overwhelmed with the urge to see her father. She knew she ought to be mourning Aunt Em—telling stories that brought back the past, made it real once again, but she couldn't. She didn't want to make the past real again. She only wanted to see her dad in the present, touch his face, look into his eyes. At that moment she missed him terribly and completely. She needed to smell him, as she did on the train station platform, as she did when she was a little girl, sitting on his lap, jamming her nose against his neck and telling him, "You smell like Daddy."

Siân found her brother Edward in a corner of the living room, looking younger than his fourteen years, uncomfortable in a blue blazer, pressed gray pants, a red and blue striped clip-on tie. He was standing with another boy his age, dressed exactly the same, the same short haircut, Brylcreemed, parted on the side. They looked as if they were pretending to be adults. Edward's friend walked away when Siân arrived.

"Where's dad?" she asked her brother.

"Outside for a smoke. That's my guess."

"I thought he quit. He told me he quit."

Edward shrugged. "That's what he says. But he smokes as much as ever. Now he's just sneaky about it."

Siân's mother walked in, setting a steaming casserole on the table. She paused, pivoted, and headed briskly towards the kitchen—as if she's running a restaurant, Siân thought.

"What do you think?" Siân said to Edward.

"About what?"

"About Aunt Em."

Edward shook his head. "I don't think about her. I just don't remember."

FROM THE UNLIT BACKYARD PORCH, it took a minute before Siân could see her parents standing close together in the yard, obscured in the evening dusk. A cigarette flared, casting a moment's glow over her father's face, his eyes closed. He dropped the cigarette and stepped on it, dragging his foot back. She couldn't remember ever seeing her parents in such an intimate moment: no dishes being washed or dried, no vegetables chopped or TV watched. Siân walked quietly down the steps leading to the yard, not wanting to interrupt but compelled to go forward. She stopped when she heard a sharp sound, the gasp of something caught in a trap. She stared into the dark. A creature had been hurt, somewhere in this yard. Then she realized that her father had made the sound. He hunched his shoulders, slumped his head forward. She'd never heard him cry before. How could that sound belong to him?

"Go on," Siân's mother said, her words cutting into the quiet scene. "Cry all you want, but it won't change a thing. Not the past. Not the present. Oh, poor you. Always poor, poor you."

Her father sucked in a deep breath. "Not for me." He gasped out the words. "Not for me."

"Then who? For me? I don't think so. For Edward? Siân? Emily? Are you crying for Emily? No. It's all for you."

"I loved her."

"So you say."

Siân heard another sharp intake of breath before her father got control.

"She gave my life meaning."

"No," Siân's mother said. "No, she didn't. She was as selfish as you. You deserved each other."

Siân's father dropped to his knees, his hands on either side of his head, as if to hold it steady. Her mother stared at him for a moment, then started off at a brisk pace toward the porch, stopping abruptly when she saw Siân. She strode past her daughter, up the stairs, into the house.

Siân faced her father, still on his knees, hands now over his eyes, surrendering himself to grief. He took a deep breath, his shoulders sinking with a long exhale. Siân watched him stagger to his feet. He ran fingers through his thinning hair.

"Dad!" she called. "Daddy!"

And when he turned, she ran to him, her arms reaching out.

Photograph

ARTHUR SQUATTED by the fireplace to warm his hands. The room felt comfortable for the first time he could remember—with sunlight streaming through the windows now that the heavy curtains and lace had been stripped away. His parents had always set the thermostat at sixty-two in winter, and down to fifty-five at night. "Waste not want not," his father would say if Arthur complained when visiting on a cold February afternoon. The old man wore a winter coat until his elbows poked through. Arthur's mother could be upset for days by an ink stain on a shirt that, in her words, "can't be made right." After his mother died three years earlier, of a cancer that spread through her body long before the diagnosis, his father kept the room even colder—punishing himself, Arthur thought, for daring to outlive his wife. "You have enough money to make yourself comfortable," Arthur would tell him. "And you know I'll always help out." "I *am* comfortable," he'd insist. "It's *you* who's not comfortable"—which in a way, of course, was true. After arriving that morning with his family to finish packing up, Arthur cranked the thermostat to seventy-five and lit a fire with the remaining scraps of firewood, though it was a mild and sunny early October afternoon.

The movers had hauled out the furniture, which would go up for auction next week. It was unnerving to see the empty room, the bare windows, as if clothing had been pulled off a body. The room seemed twice its normal size—and with sunlight flooding the space, it had become strange, nothing like the close, cold room in which he'd done his schoolwork and listened to the radio as a child and teenager. Now the room could finally breathe. How his parents had loved their hulking couch and matching chairs, purchased on an installment plan. Today, when the movers carried them out, they were scuffed and worn, the brown-and-green plaid faded to dull brown. Arthur had offered many times to buy his father a new set. "Until it's broken," his father would say, "it's not." The Barcalounger facing the TV with rabbit ear antenna *was* in fact broken—the footrest wouldn't retract. But his father had been most comfortable while sitting in that ancient, shabby thing, which is where Arthur found him after the stroke that killed him, a baseball game flickering on TV.

After Arthur's mother had passed, his father lived alone in the house. His once sharp memory blurred—and he compensated by talking and doing less. Soon he couldn't twist lids off jars or carry out the garbage, though as a railway worker he'd prided himself on his powerful hands and arms and had been the arm wrestling champion of his local at the Utica station, finally bested at age fifty by the youngest union member.

More and more Arthur had relied on clues to tell him how his father was doing. Arthur knew his father had developed an eye problem when he gave up reading the paper—cataracts, it turned out. A pillow and bed sheets stored in the closet by the front door told Arthur that his father had taken to sleeping on the couch because he couldn't manage the stairs. So Arthur hired a woman to clean house each Saturday and cook his father an evening meal. Many times Arthur had tried to persuade him to move to a nursing home—for the companionship and regular meals. But his father insisted that he wouldn't survive away from this house—his first and only in America, where he'd raised his child, where his wife exhaled her last breath.

CONNIE AND THE KIDS were waiting out in the car, and the only things left to pack were photographs on the wall above the fireplace. The largest was of Arthur's father's parents standing in front of their terraced house in the north Wales village of Corris, dressed for Sunday chapel. The photo to the right showed his mother's parents, on chairs in a garden, also in formal, dark clothes. The third photograph was of a narrow street, deserted except for a man standing by a horse and cart and a cluster of boys outside the door to a shop. The man's cap and buttoned-up jacket were identical to what the boys wore. He held the horse's reins with one hand. He seemed relaxed—despite the buttoned-up jacket and tie—and stared directly at the photographer. Arthur's parents never explained why this photograph deserved its place of honor above the fireplace. It showed the high street in their village, but they didn't remember who took the photograph or when or why. Arthur once asked his father if the man in the photograph was a relative, maybe a cousin or uncle.

"No idea," his father had replied from his Barcalounger. He was reading the newspaper. "Just a man. Just someone."

"But Taid and Nain must have known him. Didn't everyone know everyone in that village?"

His father set down the newspaper and got up to examine the photograph. "No clue," he said finally. "Just a man. A man in the village."

The fourth and last photograph was of Arthur after his baptism, outfitted in a long white gown, sitting on a velvet pillow by a vase of flowers—surely props in the photographer's studio. That was the only hard evidence that Arthur had ever lived a different life in a different place—his early childhood in Wales. He'd been baptized in a village chapel. His mother had pushed him down the high street in a pram—to the baker, the green grocer, the chemist, the butcher. He took his first steps on a slate floor.

He played in the streets. He visited grandparents in their identical terraced houses. He had friends—and together they would have spoken a language that remained with Arthur only as isolated words: *aderyn*—bird; *llwy*—spoon. Soon after his fifth birthday he was with his parents on the Britannia, sailing from Liverpool to New York. He recollected nothing of that early life—not his grandparents, the chapel, the high street, the ocean liner, not even New York harbor—he knew of the Statue of Liberty only from TV.

Arthur had taken one trip to Wales with his parents the year before he married, when he'd turned twenty-eight, by airplane. The trip was a chance for them to show off their successful son, demonstrating that they'd made the right decision in leaving Wales. But as it turned out, the relatives who'd stayed behind had done well also—better than well if the measure was the state of their cars or the front parlor furniture. The post war years had been difficult, certainly, but in the 1950s and '60s jobs could be had in Swansea and Cardiff, or London, Liverpool, and Birmingham, where his cousins and uncles and aunts now lived. His grandparents had long since died. None of his relatives remained in Corris, though he and his parents made a quick visit. Dark and narrow streets. Steep mountainsides with dots of sheep and thin, frothy waterfalls. Stone buildings. Small houses, small rooms. Slate everywhere—on roofs, as floors, strung together as fences. Slate the color of clouds; clouds the color of slate. A world of slate.

Staring again at the photograph of the nameless man in the village, Arthur suddenly felt that he knew the mystery man, knew him intimately in fact. Why hadn't he understood before? It was himself. It was Arthur as he would have been, as he would have looked, and dressed, and carried himself as a young man, if the family hadn't left the village.

Arthur lifted the photograph from the wall—and was startled by a bright green rectangle. Each of the remaining photographs when removed left a similar shape on the faded wallpaper. Arthur pulled out the nails from the walls with a hammer, tossing them in the cardboard box. He slipped the photographs from their frames and set the frames in the box. They seemed so fragile—slivers of life that might disintegrate at any moment. Arthur's parents told few stories about life in Wales, as if that world had faded over time like the wallpaper, drained of color and finally of substance. But his parents had been children in this village. They'd run along the narrow streets. They'd played hide-and-seek on the hillsides. They'd gazed west to the Irish Sea from the top of Cader Idris when it wasn't shrouded in clouds. They'd fallen in love and somewhere, at some time, in some private place in that village, had declared their love to each other. There was passion. They married and had a child the following year. They decided they could have a better life if they emigrated and told this to their parents. What were those conversations like? Where did they happen? Two families losing a son, a daughter, a grandson to a continent an ocean away. Not for days or a week, but for the rest of their lives. Why didn't his parents tell those stories? Weren't they the important stories?

After arranging the photographs from largest to smallest, Arthur rolled each into a scroll, which he tied with twine. He squatted in front of the fireplace and set the largest scroll on the bed of coals, watching wisps of gray smoke drift up. He saw the twine loosen, the scroll unravel—erupting into green, blue, purple flames then blackening and shriveling into itself. Then he set the other photographs on the coals and watched those also unravel and burst into flames that quickly died away.

Connie opened the door and walked in. "Art?" she said. "Are you finished? The kids are getting antsy. I thought you were nearly done."

"Yes," he said. He stood. "I'm finished now. Thanks."

"Should you throw some water on those coals?" she asked. "We won't be back for a while."

"No, it's safe," he said. "No danger."

He kneeled to tape shut the flaps on the box of frames, then stood. His eyes drifted to the rectangles on the wall.

"Are you all right?" Connie asked. "Do you feel you've said goodbye?" She slipped her arm through his. "You can stay longer if you'd like."

"I'm fine," Arthur said. "I've said goodbye."

Their five-year-old son, Kevin, ran into the room, directly to his mother, taking her hand with both of his.

"I told you to wait in the car," she said sternly. "You promised you would do that."

"I lost the game because Craig and Helen weren't playing fair," he said. "And then they ignored me even though I was asking questions." He looked around the room. "Hey," he said, "where's the old people? They're supposed to be up on that wall. They're always up there, instead of those green squares. Where'd they go?"

"Your father packed them up," Connie said. "In this box. We're taking them home with us."

"Let me see them," Kevin said.

"No," Arthur said. "Your brother and sister are waiting. We've been here long enough. It's time to go."

Kevin's faced reddened. "Let me see them," he said. "The old people. The faces that are supposed to be up there. You know who I mean. I want to see them."

Arthur could tell from his son's pursed lips and reddening cheeks that he was close to tears.

"Why can't I?" the boy said again. "Why can't I see them?"

"Open the box, Arthur," Connie said. "It'll only take a minute. He's had a tough week. We need to go home."

"We've all had a tough week, haven't we?" Arthur said sharply. "How about *my* tough week?" He felt heat rise up around his throat. "He was *my* father, remember? This was *my* house. I'm the one in the empty room trying to make sense of emptiness. I was born in that village. I'm the one taken away from everything. I'm the one no longer on that wall. Where is my home supposed to be?"

Connie looked at her husband's face closely. She picked up the cardboard box.

"Come along," she said to Kevin, who was staring at his father, lower lip trembling. "We'll take the old people home. Losing Taid was hard on everyone, but especially your dad. We need to remember that. When we get home we'll open the box, I promise."

"Then we'll feel better?" Kevin asked. "When we open the box? And dad will feel better?"

"Yes," Connie said. "Then we'll all feel better."

Transactions

"YOU'RE GOING THIS AFTERNOON. For dinner, right?" Celeste asked as they walked into the classroom on the second floor of the parish hall, the empty chairs in rows facing a blackboard. The Sunday service had just ended, so they had a few minutes alone before needing to find their parents.

Ellis nodded. "I've been going to Uncle Emyr and Aunt Winni's for dinner every Sunday as long as I can remember. Unless we're on vacation."

Celeste shut the door. On the far wall hung a portrait of Jesus with shoulder-length brown hair swept off his broad forehead and a short, trimmed beard. Old wooden bookcases were filled with bibles, bible commentaries, and hymnals, some in Welsh. They could hear the downstairs rumble of parents gathering children and saying goodbyes.

"And you'll get it?" Celeste asked. "It's the only thing in there."

"Which drawer?"

"Top drawer. I can't believe I let him have it. I don't know what I was thinking. So you'll get it?"

"I'll get it. I'll make some kind of excuse and get it. It'll be easy."

"You've been there before?"

"He doesn't let anyone in his room."

"Except me," Celeste said. Then, annoyed, she added, "Can you really do this?"

"I'll get it, no problem," Ellis said.

"And you can't tell anyone. Promise."

"I promise. Why'd you give it to him, anyway?"

Celeste shrugged. "He asked. Back when he talked to me, he asked. But now he's not talking, so I want it back."

"OK," Ellis said. "And your part of the deal. You ready?"

"Go ahead," she said. "I thought you'd never ask."

Ellis stepped closer, setting an open palm on Celeste's right breast. Celeste stared directly into Ellis's eyes until he turned his head. Through the fabric, he felt the seam of her bra. Who could he tell about this? No one. Not yet. He circled his hand. He squeezed.

"Don't do that," Celeste told him.

"Sorry," he said. "I thought girls liked that."

"We don't." She swatted his hand off and pinched his chest hard.

"Hey!" he said. "Why'd you do that?"

"So you know how it feels."

"I didn't pinch you."

"I don't care. You don't know how to be nice, that's the point." She thought about this. "Tom knows how. And how not to be nice."

"How is he not nice?"

"That's none of your business is it?"

"I'll get it for you," Ellis said, "I promise. And when I bring it back, you'll let me see. You know, without the top. See for real. The whole thing. That's what you promised."

"OK."

"Then it's a deal."

Ellis put out his hand but Celeste laughed and opened the door. "I'm not shaking your hand," she said. "That's dumb. Just go to Tom's room. Get it for me. And don't tell anyone."

AS USUAL, ELLIS AND HIS sister Kate were seated at a card table across from his cousin Tom and abutting the dinner table where his parents and Uncle Emyr and Aunt Winni sat, men on one side, women on the other. Though Tom was the tallest in the room, he had to sit at the card table with the other children. The Sunday china, with steaming casserole dishes set on trivets, was laid out on the table where the parents sat. An unspoken rule was that all passed dishes had to be returned to the adults' table. To Ellis, the tables felt like warring camps, with the adults always destined to win.

"So how's school going, Tom?" Ellis's mother asked while passing the scalloped potatoes.

"Fine," Tom said.

"Your prom's coming up soon, right, dear?"

"Yes."

"Who are you taking?"

"Don't know."

"That's because he can't decide among all the girls," Ellis's father said. "Isn't that right, Tom?"

"Dad, why do you say things like that?" Kate said, lightly scratching the rash along the bottom of her arm.

"I have to say, it's true," Ellis's uncle said gruffly. "Tom's a great one for the girls. Isn't that so, Winni?"

"Don't bring me into this," she replied as she picked up and passed a plate of buttered bread. "I have no idea. My son tells me nothing."

"Is there a sweetheart, Tom?" Ellis's father asked. "For the long haul?"

Tom shrugged.

"And you," he said to Kate. "You'll be fending off the boys soon enough. Thinking about them, are you?"

"No, she's not foolish like that," Kate's mother said. "You should leave her alone. And thinking's not the same as doing."

"But a nod's as good as a wink," Ellis's uncle said, and he winked at Kate. He turned to Ellis, who was staring at his plate in hopes of not attracting attention. "And this boy's thinking thoughts. Aren't you, Ellis *bach*?"

"Thoughts?" Ellis said to his uncle. "What thoughts?"

"Shall we talk about today's sermon?" Ellis's mother interjected. "Isn't that a healthier topic? Ellis, what did you think of it?"

He stared at his mother and shook his head.

"Can you at least tell us what it was about?"

Ellis could only recall fragments. A sycamore tree. A tax man. "Tax," he said. "People angry about tax."

"Tax?" Ellis's father laughed out loud. "That's ridiculous. No one'd give a sermon on tax. Have you ever heard a sermon on tax, Emyr?"

"No, never."

"It was about humility," Ellis's mother said. "How even tax collectors can be humble. How we . . . climb out of a tree and . . . invite the Lord into our house."

"Can I be excused?" Ellis asked.

"No," his father said. "We haven't had pudding."

"I need to use the bathroom."

"You used the bathroom at home—I know because I had to wait. You and your sister live in that bathroom. Might as well put beds in there."

"You may leave," Ellis's mother said. "But when you've finished, return to the dinner table. There'll be no TV. This is family time."

IN THE BATHROOM Ellis examined himself in the mirror, wishing he were taller and his face more narrow, like Tom's—with a brooding aura that girls found attractive. They were cousins, so why didn't they look more alike? He closed his eyes, enjoying the quiet. He wondered how long it would be until pudding and tea were served, and how long after that until his family would leave. How many more questions would he be asked that he didn't know how to answer? Why didn't they talk to Kate instead?

Ellis washed and dried his hands. He glanced again at his face in the mirror, flushed the toilet, though he hadn't used it, and walked into the hall. He listened to muffled conversation from the dining room, his father's and Uncle Emyr's voices—tenor and bass—the loudest, as usual, arguing some point of city politics, church gossip, or family history.

He took a few steps along the hall and opened Tom's bedroom door, shutting it soundlessly behind him. A bed, unexpectedly neat. A desk under a window. Tom's Sunday jacket, shirt, tie, and pants folded on a plastic chair. Against one wall, a half-empty bookcase. Next to the closet, a beat-up dresser, the veneer peeling off one side. Ellis pulled out the top drawer. It was empty. Completely empty. He ran fingers across the bottom panel, as if he might touch something invisible.

There was no other dresser. Why, he wondered, would the top drawer be empty? Didn't Celeste say the *top* drawer? Now he couldn't clearly remember what she'd said. He pulled out the second drawer: socks and underwear. He rummaged. He yanked open the third drawer: shirts and white T-shirts, neatly folded, unlike his own dresser drawers where everything was balled up and messy. His mother would fold the clothes, but somehow the folding disarranged into chaos over the course of a week. What will I do? Ellis thought. What will I tell Celeste? It's got to be here somewhere. He pulled out the bottom drawer. And there, to his surprise, was more underwear—but girls' underwear, fifteen or twenty pairs, pink and white. Moving a hand through the heap, he found and pulled out a sheet of paper—a neatly-written list of names: Kate was last and Celeste second to last.

The door opened, and Ellis turned to see Tom, filling the doorway. "What the hell are you doing?" he said, stepping in.

"I lost something."

"Lost something? In my bedroom? What?"

"A baseball card. I thought maybe . . ."

"Tell me what you're really doing, do you hear me? Why are you in my room going through my stuff? Tell me or I'll break your arm. I don't care about your parents. I'll twist your arm till it cracks."

Ellis dropped the paper in the drawer. "I can't tell you."

"What are you talking about?" Tom shut the door. "You'll tell me, or I'll hurt you worse than you've ever been hurt."

"It's Celeste," Ellis said.

"Celeste Jones? From church?"

Ellis nodded. "She told me to get something. She wants it back."

Tom smiled, understanding. "I don't give those back."

"Can I just take *hers* back?"

"Why?"

"I . . . she said she'd pay me. She said she'd give five dollars. She wants it back because you won't talk to her."

"I don't talk to any of them. I talk, then I stop talking."

"Just let me have one."

"Why should I?"

"Because you're my cousin. We're family."

"That's true," Tom said. "Can't deny that. Except there's a problem. I don't like you, and I don't like your family."

"You don't?"

"No."

"Then why's Kate's name on your list?"

This surprised Tom, who thought a moment before saying, "Anyone can be on the list. I don't have to like them."

"What's it for?"

"None of your business," Tom snapped. "You're making my business your business. But you're nothing to me, so that can't happen." He looked closely at Ellis, then at the pulled-open dresser drawer. "OK, we can make a deal, since you're family. Ever watch that show, *Let's Make a Deal?*"

"No."

"It's about weird deals. So let's do one: I give you something, you give me something."

"What?"

"Something you're wearing. Your underwear."

Ellis waited for Tom to laugh and say it was a joke. A joke that Ellis didn't get, like one his father might tell at dinner. But Tom was serious.

"Don't worry, cousin. No one will know. How could anyone know? It's just a transaction. Something that was yours becomes mine. And something that was mine becomes yours. It happens all the time. It makes the world go round."

Ellis brought to mind the coming Wednesday night choir practice, the Sunday school room where he'd arranged to meet Celeste. Then he thought about his underwear being kept in Tom's drawer, mixed with ones belonging to girls Tom knew. Transactions. He started to feel that he might throw up.

"Tom!" a voice called out. "Ellis! Where are you?" It was Aunt Winni. "Rice pudding is served!"

Tom stepped further into the room. "Be quick," he told Ellis. "It'll just take a second. And I'll like you better afterwards. We'll hang out."

"OK." Ellis hung his head for a moment. Then he turned, snatched up a pair of underwear and the list, jammed them in his pocket, and lunged past Tom to the door, bursting out to the hall. "Coming!" he shouted. "Sorry!"

Ellis plopped into his chair in front of a bowl of rice pudding. He set a hand over the lump in his pocket.

"Did you forget how the toilet works?" his father asked.

"No," Ellis said. "I didn't."

Tom walked in and took his seat. He stared, unsmiling, at Ellis.

"What were you two talking about?" Uncle Emyr asked. "What's the big secret? Were you gossiping like a couple of girls?"

"Ah, girls," Ellis's father said. "The secret that's not a secret."

"Why do you always say that kind of thing?" Kate said. "Tom has other things to think about."

"And do you want to excuse yourself, Katie *fach*?" her father said. "And have a private word with Tom?"

"Alun," Ellis mother said sharply. "That's enough. They're cousins. There's no need to make trouble where there's no trouble. Please, let's eat our pudding."

WHEN ELLIS ENTERED THE ROOM, Celeste was standing in front of the blackboard in a pleated blue skirt, her white blouse buttoned to the neck.

"Did you get it?" she asked.

Ellis nodded.

"Where is it?"

"It wasn't easy," he said. "And Tom knows I took it."

"I don't care what Tom knows," she said. "I don't care about him anymore. Now give it to me."

He pulled crumpled white underwear from his pants pocket. It could be hers, Ellis told himself. There's no saying it isn't.

She held it up, her expression blank.

"I didn't think you'd bring it," she said finally.

"I almost got my arm broken," Ellis said. "And there's worse that could happen when I go back next week. Tom won't forget. He's meaner than I ever knew. So now it's your turn. We have a deal. Dad's waiting, so we have to be quick."

"All right," she said. "But no squeezing. Promise?"

"Promise," Ellis said.

Celeste opened her purse, but before dropping in the underwear she noticed something and examined the underwear more closely.

"This label," she said. "It's wrong. This isn't from Woolworths. This isn't mine."

"Yes, it's yours," Ellis said. "Definitely, definitely yours."

"No, it's definitely not mine. What are you up to? You bought this somewhere, didn't you? Or stole your sister's. That's sick, that's really sick."

"I didn't buy it, and it's not Kate's. I've never seen Kate's underwear. At least I don't think so."

"You don't think so? What does that mean? Where's this from?"

"I don't know," Ellis said. "But it could be yours."

"Could be? *Could* be?"

"He's got a drawer full. Like a collection. A weird hobby. That one could be yours. Yours was in there somewhere, and I might have gotten it. I sneaked into his room. I found the drawer. I did everything you asked. So now you need to take your top off, like you promised." He brought to mind the white bra holding soft breasts beneath her buttoned-up blouse. "You promised."

Celeste stared at him, uncomprehending. "A *drawer* full?"

"And a list of names."

"Whose names?"

"I don't know. Girls' names."

"Do you have it?"

He nodded.

"Give it to me."

Ellis produced the paper. "Transactions," he said. "That's all. A deal."

Celeste scanned the sheet and stuffed it in her purse. She grabbed the back of Ellis's head and smashed the underwear over his mouth and nose. "Is this what you want?" she shouted. "Is this is what idiot boys dream about? OK, your dream's come true. It's all yours."

Celeste tossed the underwear to the floor. "Tom will get his," she said. "I'll figure out how. He'll wish he'd never set eyes on me."

ALONE IN THE CLASSROOM, Ellis picked up the underwear with a thumb and index finger. He thought his nose might be bleeding, or his lip, but they were OK when he carefully felt them. He'd blown his chance, completely, and there wouldn't be another. Not with Celeste anyway. And no other girl would be like Celeste. Tom, he knew, was planning to do something very bad to him. Tom was thinking right now about what would hurt him the most.

I'll bring it to dinner next Sunday, Ellis thought. I'll get Tom alone somehow and give it back, and every Sunday from then on he'll ignore me like always.

"But maybe . . . ," he said aloud.

He thought about his own bedroom and the bottom drawer in his desk that he never used except for pencils and erasers, and a pad of paper. The best hiding place in the room. Then he stuffed the underwear in his back pocket.

He could do this, but he'd have to be careful. He'd have to make sure that no one would find out.

Dreaming of Home

OLD LLEW could not fit the key into the lock of his front door, though he'd opened it a thousand times over the years. Lately the lock had developed a mind of its own, especially at night, shifting left when Llew moved his key right, then jerking right when he went left.

"Damn you!" Llew shouted. "*Diawl!*" Then he jabbed the key with eyes shut, somehow stabbing through the keyhole.

"People trying to sleep!" a voice shouted from the upstairs apartment. "*Please* be quiet!"

Llew closed the door as silently as he could. He'd drunk half a jug of Thunderbird after breakfast, a dozen draft beers through the afternoon and evening at Riley's, and was looking forward to the hefty dram of Powers that helped bring on sleep. He dropped his jacket to the floor. In the kitchen, he allowed himself an extra-large measure, splattering some across the countertop. "Steady on," he told himself. "It doesn't grow on trees." In the parlor, he turned on his portable TV, set his whiskey on the stained Formica side table, mottled with intersecting rings the same circumference as his glass. He eased himself carefully into his old reclining chair.

A CBS News program reported on a predawn mortar assault by the Viet Cong against the Bien Hoa air base, twelve miles north of Saigon. A reporter spoke from the scene, quoting the army's promise to hunt down and kill or capture the attackers. Llew stared at the

flickering black-and-white images of Vietnamese and American soldiers, trying to follow what was being said.

LLEW STOOD in six inches of brackish water, shoulder-to-shoulder
in the trench with his comrades, bayonet fixed, awaiting the order.
It was raining steadily with dawn diffusing around them—enough
light to see a trench rat by his boot, gnawing the edge of an empty
ration can. Ahead of Llew was scrubland pocked with muddy
craters—and beyond that the German barbed wire, sandbags, and
trenches.

"Too much bloody light now," Dai Siop muttered on Llew's
left. "What're the buggers waiting for?"

Ten minutes later, the order was shouted, and Llew and his
comrades scrambled over the top of the trench into daylight and
an eruption of gunfire.

IT WAS DIFFICULT TO SEE with the fog settled in, but Llew could
make out the shapes of his nearest comrades—Dai Siop, Henry
Tonmawr, Dic Cadwalladr, Jacob *bach*—some with bullet wounds
in the head and chest, others with limbs blown off from mortar fire.
They'd fallen back, or crawled back, to this place. All dead, or about
to die. When a rat climbed onto Dai Siop's face, Llew tried to crawl
to his friend, but found his legs didn't work. He looked down at
his chest where a bullet had blasted through, soaking his uniform
dark red. He hoisted himself to his knees and clasped his shaking
hands in front of him, feeling the urge to pray as he'd prayed in
Jerusalem Chapel as a child in Blaen Cwm, fervently, with unques-
tioning faith, his mother and father on either side in the pew. But
though his lips moved, he couldn't produce words. So he sat down
in the cold muck, closed his eyes, and said to himself, *Now I'll know
what it's like to die.*

But he didn't die. He opened his eyes. An old man emerged from the fog, trudging towards him. Llew thought this must be his older self, the one who survived the war and recovered in a hospital, who'd returned to his village then emigrated to America and somehow, through processes he could not remember, became the person he was.

The old man drew closer.

"*Tada?*" Llew whispered. Then he shouted with certainty, "*Tada!*" He was overwhelmed that his father had found him in the bloody trench among the decimated bodies of his comrades.

"Yes," his father said. "It's me."

"Take me home! Take me back to Blaen Cwm," Llew called out, raising his arms as if he were a child who could be lifted and carried away.

"But you *are* home, my boy," his father said.

"No!" Llew shouted. "This is not where I belong."

"Are you sure?" His father shook his head. "This is where you always return. So really, it must be your home."

"Take me away," Llew pleaded. "I can't stay here. I'll die."

Llew's father glanced up at the sky, which could have been dawn or dusk. "You won't," he said. "You'll lie down in this muck, unconscious. The battle will start up again, but a medic will find his way here. He'll put fingers on your throat and feel a pulse. He'll stitch your wound. He'll inject morphine. Then there's the hospital, the painful healing in that room crowded with wounded men on cots, and in time, the bus dropping you off on the high street, the night at the Three Feathers with the men asking to see your scars. Within a year, you and your brother will take the ship from Liverpool to New York—all that seasickness. Your months in the basement room in Remsen as you looked for work. You were a milkman for a year, weren't you? Didn't you write that to me?

Then your flat on Sunset Avenue and a real job as a bricklayer. But you never belonged in this country, did you? In a sense you were never really here. For the years we had remaining, your mother and I missed you terribly—we never recovered from losing our sons to America. There's much that you'll do, but throughout all the changes, one thing will be constant: you'll always remember your home."

And Llew's father turned and trudged back through the muck the way he'd come, disappearing into a vapor that would soon be burned off by the sun.

OLD LLEW blinked into the glare of the TV test pattern. He reached for his whiskey but touched the bare table. Leaning over, he saw the upturned glass by a dark splotch on the carpet. He'd had a dream, he thought—he was certain he'd had a dream but couldn't remember what happened in it, or where he was. Then a fragment arrived: his arms reaching to his father.

"Dreaming of home," Old Llew said. "That's it! Dreaming of *Tada* and where I belong. The terrace house on Heol y Garth. Blaen Cwm. The hills. Not this bad joke with no punch line. My *real* home."

He closed his eyes, murmuring to himself over and over the words *Tada* and *home*, hoping that they had the power to return him to the dreamworld—the only place where he truly belonged.

Prodigal Son

WHEN A THIN, SMARTLY DRESSED MAN in a dark suit and tie knocked on the front door during the early evening to ask if Daniel was in, John Gwilym Morris was not entirely surprised. At last, he thought, at long last it's come to this.

"Daniel doesn't live here," John Gwilym said, straightening his back. "He's been gone for two weeks. He's found his own place."

The man peered into the hallway. "He's not at his own place. So we figured he'd gone home."

"I told you, he doesn't live here. Now tell me your business. How much does he owe you?"

"He doesn't owe me anything, Mr. Morris. I just need to talk with him."

"You're from the police then? Can I see your identification?"

"Identification?" The man smiled. "I got no identification."

"What happened to Daniel?"

"That's what I want to know," the man said. "It's what my boss wants to know. Your kid's in . . . well, he's in hot water. He's developed some bad habits."

"I know all about his bad habits."

"I don't think so. Not these. The sooner he shows up to straighten things out, the better."

"Shows up where?"

"He knows where." The man shook his head, almost sadly. "He's not gone far. Where does a nineteen-year-old go? Sooner or later he'll show up because you're all he's got. That's how it is. And when he does show up, he should call me. He's got my number." The man leaned forward. "Tell him to call Joseph. He shouldn't talk to anyone but Joseph."

John Gwilym's wife Beti joined her husband. "Do we have a guest?" she asked.

"No," John Gwilym said. "He's just leaving."

"Remember, Mr. Morris, this is serious," the man said. "This is not playing around. I can't help your son unless he calls me. And he needs to do it soon."

Beti put a hand over her mouth. "Dear Lord," she said. "Oh my dear Lord. What is he saying? What does he mean?"

"You need to leave," John Gwilym told his visitor. "Leave us right now."

SINCE DANIEL WAS BORN, John Gwilym had concentrated on one aspect of being a father—discipline. His son had strict instructions for when to go to bed, when to rise in the morning, which chores to complete each day. No television during the week except an hour on Saturday. He attended Sunday school, the regular service and the weekly youth choir, despite being tone deaf with a weak singing voice. He competed in *eisteddfodau* recitations, though he couldn't remember more than three lines of poetry no matter how many hours he spent repeating them aloud. He wasn't simple, exactly, but the boy had difficulty reading and writing, and couldn't make a sum of two numbers without using fingers. His father required him to do homework alone in his bedroom for three hours each night to learn self-sufficiency. If he brought home a failing grade, he'd earn a whipping with a belt worn smooth with use. This was how John Gwilym had been raised by his father in Clydach Vale—though *Tad* had used a cane not a belt. Early on Beti tried to suggest that her husband's tactics might be too strict—but by the time Daniel was a teenager, she'd learned not to interfere. Despite John Gwilym's rigorous discipline, the older Daniel got, the more trouble he got into. The beatings became a weekly routine.

Sometimes he'd return from school or the local playground with a black eye or scrapes and cuts on his arms and cheeks, or ripped clothes, and John Gwilym knew he'd been fighting. Secretly he was proud that his boy never complained or named the other boy or boys involved when Beti questioned him. John Gwilym had been an amateur boxer himself—the sport was big in Clydach Vale after Tommy Farr, "The Tonypandy Terror," nearly beat Joe Louis in 1937—and he'd taught boxing skills to his son. At sixteen, Daniel was taller than his father and physically powerful. John Gwilym had come to believe that someday he and Daniel would have a real fight, not a father's one-sided whipping of a boy. A part of him looked forward to that day.

On his seventeenth birthday, Daniel didn't come home for dinner, staying out until after one in the morning. John Gwilym waited up, sitting grimly in the dining room, his belt on his lap. The boy arrived, drunk, hardly able to walk, though somehow he managed to strip off his shirt and kneel down, offering his back to his father, with head bent as if in prayer. Neither said a word. For the first time, John Gwilym examined the crisscrossed scars. Though he'd seen them proliferate over the years, he'd never before understood their significance. They made up a history of this father and son relationship, an indelible record on the boy's body. Above the scars, at the back of the boy's neck, the skin was suddenly as smooth and clear as a blank sheet of paper.

"Go on," the boy said, slurring his words. "Do it."

"No one can say I didn't try," John Gwilym told his son as he snapped the belt taut. "That's one thing they cannot say."

AT NINETEEN the boy managed to graduate from high school, but couldn't find a job. He'd sleep late, eat breakfast, and go out, claiming to be looking for work, or doing odd jobs for people never named. On the evening of Beti's thirty-seventh birthday, she and John Gwilym were having their tea and watching television in the living room. Daniel had missed supper and the birthday cake. He walked into the room at half past nine, holding out a paper bag. "Happy birthday, Mam," he mumbled.

His mother drew from the bag a small porcelain unicorn and held it up. The spiraling horn thrust out from its lowered head, its right front leg was bent and raised.

"It's lovely," she said. "So delicate. You're very thoughtful, Daniel." With a handkerchief, she wiped her eyes. "It belongs on the mantel," she added, "where everyone can see it."

John Gwilym glanced to the coffee table where his own gift, a bottle of perfume, sat on wrapping paper. He stood from his chair.

"Where did you get it?" he asked his son.

"From a store."

"Where'd you find the money?"

"I earned the money."

"Earned it? You don't have a job."

"He's doing odd jobs," Beti said. "Around the neighborhood. Isn't that right, Daniel?"

"Odd jobs indeed," John Gwilym said. "You stole that thing, didn't you? Walked into a store and put it in your pocket."

"He didn't," Beti put in. "He wouldn't have."

His wife's defense of Daniel, together with the whiskey fumes in the air and the boy's insolence, gave John Gwilym a moment of nausea. The room began turning around him. He set a hand on his stomach. Then he whipped around and shoved his wife into her chair.

"Oh yes," he hissed. "Take his side. Always taking his side. He reeks of drink, yet you take *his* side."

John Gwilym snatched the unicorn from Beti's hand and flung it at the fireplace.

The boy looked from his mother to the scattered white fragments, not seeming to understand what had happened. Then his face changed—in a moment he looked years older.

"If you touch her again," the boy snarled, "I'll kill you."

"You dare speak to me," John Gwilym said, "stinking drunk as you are."

The boy lunged, and the two began swinging fists, heedless of teacups and saucers crashing off the table while Beti wailed and pleaded, "Stop! The both of you stop. Please just stop."

One loud scream from Beti distracted Daniel long enough for John Gwilym to land a left hook on his chin. Stunned, the boy looked directly into his father's eyes before dropping heavily to the floor.

"Don't," John Gwilym commanded when Beti rushed to her son. "Don't touch him. Let him awaken in his blood. Then maybe he'll look around himself and understand what I've been trying to teach."

Beti left for their bedroom, weeping. John Gwilym stared down at his son, curled in the fetal position. In the bathroom, John Gwilym washed his face and hands and staunched his bleeding nose with toilet paper—not knowing if the blood that turned the water pink was Daniel's or his own, or both.

THE NEXT MORNING DANIEL WAS out of the house before dawn, leaving a brown stain where his mouth had pressed against the carpet.

He didn't return that night, or the next. On the third night he arrived with an empty suitcase as his parents were eating dinner, wearing the same clothes as when he had left—blood-spattered, rank with sweat.

"I've got an apartment," he announced.

"No," his mother said. "We . . ."

"Enough," John Gwilym said. He stood. "I've had enough. Leave if you want. But you will take nothing from this house to pawn or sell. Nothing from your room. Nothing from anywhere. You'll see that people out in the world are not kind. If you borrow from them, they'll want money back with interest. If they help you, they'll own you. Your family is all you've got. You'll learn some lessons out in the world, and you'll return to me on your knees. And then you'll treat me like a father."

Through a window facing the street, John Gwilym watched Daniel toss the empty suitcase into a car idling at the curb and jump in after it. He wondered, briefly, who was driving that car.

WHEN DANIEL HAD BEEN OUT OF THE HOUSE and out of contact for a week, John Gwilym thought for the first time that his son might have left the city. What would he gain by staying? He might be heading west to Buffalo, Cleveland, or Chicago. Or south to the sun and warmth of Florida. He might be on a Greyhound with a desert landscape rushing by. Soon he might reach a great ocean. Such an escape was what John Gwilym had envisioned for himself after Beti told him she was pregnant. Just get on a bus with only the clothes on your back and leave Clydach Vale. For Cardiff. For London. For New York. Maybe San Francisco. Leave everything— house, family, memories. All expectations. All familiar faces. Everything that prevents you from being who you are. It could be done. It could be what Daniel had done.

After dinner on the day the man who called himself Joseph had come by, Beti asked if they should tell the police that Daniel was missing.

"No," John Gwilym said. "There's nothing the police can do."

"Then can we look for him ourselves? We could use the car. I feel sure he's close by."

"He's far away, or he's hiding," John Gwilym told her, sternly. "Hiding from that man, or whoever that man works for. Do you think we'd see Daniel walking down a street? He doesn't want to be seen. He owes that man something. He's afraid of that man."

When John Gwilym stepped into the kitchen for a glass of water before going to bed, he saw his wife with the phone to her ear. She set the phone in its cradle with a trembling hand. "There's no answer," she said. "No answer again." She began crying softly.

"You phoned him?"

She nodded.

"So you have a phone number? For where he's staying?"

She nodded again.

"He gave you a number, and you've phoned him before," John Gwilym said, incredulous. "You spoke with him, yet never told me."

"He's not answering the phone," she replied simply.

John Gwilym took a deep breath and closed his eyes. After exhaling, he slapped his wife so hard she collapsed to the floor.

"You're the one," he told her—crumpled on the carpet, hands protecting her head. "You're responsible. He'd have come home soon enough. He'd have given up his ways. But no, you had to phone him, didn't you? Coddle the boy. Pamper him in secret. No wonder he hasn't come back to us. It's your fault. It's all because of you."

BY THE NEXT MORNING—a Sunday—a purple welt had erupted across Beti's cheek. So instead of going to church, she sat in a chair by the kitchen phone, covering the welt with a damp cloth. John Gwilym scrutinized the newspaper. Nothing about Daniel had been reported—in the paper or on the radio or the television. But the next evening as they prepared for bed, the phone rang.

"Mr. Morris?"

"Who's this? Is this Joseph?"

"Who I am doesn't matter. Your son's coming home, that's the point. Tomorrow night. We've cleared up everything. He told me to say he misses you both."

"Home?" John Gwilym said. "He's coming here? What time?"

But the line had gone dead.

When John Gwilym gave his wife the news, she stared at him without speaking.

"Did you hear me?" John Gwilym said. "The man told me that Daniel is coming here, tomorrow night."

"I'll make a roast lamb," Beti said, rubbing her hands on her apron. "And new potatoes. And a trifle. He's loved trifle since he was a boy." Then she looked frightened, and gently pressed fingertips on her purple, puffed-up cheek.

"Why can't he come tonight?" she asked. "Why can't he come now?"

"I don't know," John Gwilym said.

IT WAS raining as John Gwilym drove home from his job at the brewery. Beti had made the trifle and roasted the lamb and potatoes, but when Daniel hadn't arrived by seven, John Gwilym insisted that they eat. "Keep a plate in the oven," he said. "He'll eat when he gets here."

When they'd finished dinner, the rain had diminished to a drizzle, and John Gwilym carried a chair from the dining room to the covered front porch, and a blanket for the evening chill. Beti disappeared for twenty minutes, returning with makeup caked over the welt on her face.

"Will someone drive him?" she asked. "Or is he walking?"

"I wasn't told," John Gwilym said.

For the first time in his life, John Gwilym felt fear when thinking of his son. He was certain that Daniel was capable of doing terrible things. He was big enough and strong enough. He was good with his fists—John Gwilym had been like that at Daniel's age, having gotten into more fights than he could count. John Gwilym knew he'd been lucky with that left hook the one time they'd fought. He doubted he'd be lucky the next time.

"It's cold on the porch, and damp," he said to his wife. "You should wait inside."

"I can't," she said. "I need to see him as soon as he's here."

"Don't you think he and I should talk first? I might have to explain . . ." He drifted off.

"Please. I couldn't bear to wait."

"Go in the house," John Gwilym commanded. "There'll be a misunderstanding if he sees you before we talk."

"Tell him whatever you wish," Beti said. "Then bring him to me. Don't lose him again."

THAT EVENING not many cars drove down the street: an old pickup belonging to neighbors two houses to the left; a station wagon packed with teenagers, their voices rising above a song from the radio. A man with an umbrella walked by, his small dog straining on its leash. After a while, it ceased to drizzle, the air now eerily calm. Then, at nearly eleven, a black Cadillac raced onto the street, screeching to a stop in front of John Gwilym's porch. A back door opened and a naked body was shoved out onto the curb. A hand yanked the door shut and the car sped off, tires squealing. John Gwilym ran to the body.

An oily rag had been stuffed in Daniel's mouth, hair torn from his scalp, blood splattered over his face and shoulders, bruises and cuts up and down his body. His wrists were bound with wire. When John Gwilym pulled out the rag, Daniel groaned. John Gwilym cradled his son's head with an arm. He ran fingers over the blood-stiffened hair. He looked carefully at his son's face—those long, dark eyelashes, the high forehead. The boy opened his eyes, closed them, opened them again, focusing on his father. A violent spasm rippled through him. And he closed his eyes.

"No!" John Gwilym shouted. Then, more quietly, "No, no, no. Not like this. Not like this."

A light came on upstairs in the house across the street. In the distance, a police siren started up.

"Daniel," John Gwilym whispered by his son's bruised, swollen ear. "You know me, don't you? Don't you know me, Daniel? Don't you know who I am?"

He watched for a sign that he'd been heard—a flutter of eyelids, a nod—but there was only stillness and the siren's wail.

Box

REV. PRICE slowed his car to a crawl down the stretch of Holland Avenue between Parkside Court and Van Vorst Street because of a dog—a large, black dog that someone in this neighborhood let outside to run loose each morning. It wasn't mistreated and wasn't dangerous—plenty of children walking to school would stop and pet the dog, which appeared to live for affection, running up to present its head with ears pulled back, obedient in *sit* position, tail wagging frantically. The problem was that the dog did not understand the boundary between curb and road, so to reach a faraway, familiar child, it would bolt down or across Holland Avenue, oblivious to oncoming traffic. Just the previous week, Rev. Price had narrowly avoided hitting the dog head-on with a last minute swerve. For this poor creature, love had no boundaries, no restrictions, though Rev. Price was certain that one day the dog would dart towards love only to be struck down by a car or truck arriving— from the dog's point of view—out of nowhere.

He scanned left and right, then sighted the creature, not bounding after a child but statue-still on its haunches in front of the house where Rachel Pritchard had lived with her grandson Roland. Most mornings Rev. Price would see the old lady on a rocking chair on the front porch of that house, blanket over her knees, shawl around her shoulders, staring at the sidewalk and street and the neighbors across the street. He would wave, and she would raise her bony hand in response. She would have known the dog, as it would have known her. Mrs. Pritchard had died in her bedroom three days earlier, age eighty-nine, after refusing to eat for a month. And this, Rev. Price assumed, explained why the dog had, for the moment, given up his love-quests and stationed himself like a sentinel, attuned to an absence, a sad realignment in his world-without-boundaries.

Rev. Price knew the Pritchard family story as fully as he knew the stories of every family in his parish. He knew the myriad ways the body must fail: pneumonia, emphysema, heart attack, stroke, cancer, aneurism. And worst of all, the unexpected death of the young. The Phillips child, drowned in Hinckley reservoir. Richard Bowen, killed far from his parish in Vietnam. There had been one suicide since Rev. Price arrived at Bethesda Church eleven years ago, and a young man was committed to Marcy State after electro-shock didn't cure him.

Roland Pritchard's story, however, was simple. An only child orphaned when his parents died in a car accident, he had lived with his grandmother until attending college for an accounting degree. He was hired by the Utica Savings Bank and moved back into his grandmother's house, returning to his old bedroom, sleeping—Rev. Price imagined—in the single bed he'd slept in as a child. He and his grandmother lived in that house together for another fourteen years. A woman aging and dying is itself a plain story, a pure story, no matter the complicating details of how, when, and where. Today, Roland was alone—with three bedrooms, a front parlor, a dining room, a living room, a kitchen all to himself. The simple stories in that house would from now on be only about him.

Though Roland's car was parked in the driveway, the blinds were drawn over the windows of the Pritchard home as Rev. Price drove by. The rocking chair—unused for many weeks—had been removed from the porch, which now seemed to have lost its purpose, like a frame without a photograph. Earlier in the week he'd met with Roland and Evans the funeral director to sort out arrangements. This afternoon he was to meet Roland in his office at the church. What would he say to give comfort? Could he rise above the platitudes?

REV. PRICE motioned Roland to the couch while he sat in the padded chair behind his desk. Though dark semi-circles had gathered under Roland's eyes, he otherwise looked the same—dressed in the blue blazer he wore to church, with gray, pressed slacks and black polished shoes, white shirt and somber striped tie. The reverend smiled. Roland was always presentably dressed.

Rev. Price visited his most elderly parishioners each week if possible—and he'd generally set aside Saturday afternoon for tea with Roland's grandmother. During these visits Roland would join them for one cup only, demurring when Rev. Price mentioned some church activity he might consider joining. Mrs. Prichard's talk was all about the weather, or complaints about neighbors, whom she scrutinized and judged from her rocking chair with a nineteenth-century strictness. Occasionally Rev. Price would catch himself not listening to her words but staring at her mouth, fringed with sparse gray whiskers and emptied of all but a few stumps of teeth, so her thin, pale lips curled over her gums as she talked. If he asked a question, it had to be loudly and slowly, or she'd interrupt with "What's that?" or "Say again?"

When his grandmother's chatter slowed and finally paused, Roland would ask Rev. Price about his son and wife, or his pastoral work at the Presbyterian Home, or his thoughts on the anti-war movement. Roland seemed interested in what Rev. Price had to say, though he would soon guide conversation back to his grandmother's concerns and then excuse himself—he had a letter to write or bills to pay. Where would he go? Rev. Price had wondered. To his bedroom no doubt, the only room that was fully his own—leaving the reverend and Mrs. Pritchard to chat over another cup of tea from the pot Roland had brewed. He always wished Roland would stay, because his simple presence made the small—and small-minded—talk of his grandmother more bearable. Given the obligations and conditions of his life, Roland had never married, and Rev. Price thought this a wise choice. But how he must long for companionship, the reverend thought, for someone outside himself and his grandmother and this conventional house they had shared. Rev. Price felt he'd developed a relationship with Roland, defined within narrow limits but real enough—a connection he hoped would continue.

"HOW ARE YOU ROLAND?" Rev. Price asked. "How are you holding up?"

"As well as can be expected."

"It's never easy," Rev. Price said. "And your grandmother was so poorly those last weeks. Did you manage to find some help? That young nurse I recommended?"

"No, no. Nain wouldn't tolerate strangers in the home. It was difficult enough for her to accept church women, though they managed to get a bit of broth into her now and again."

"I heard that," Rev. Price said. "I made a point to ask."

"She always welcomed your visits. You were kind to her."

"I'm glad to hear you say that, Roland."

"I know I . . . never stayed long. But Nain required time with you alone. She truly enjoyed having you to herself—which must have been trying at times."

"You needn't apologize. Your grandmother and I had plenty to talk about. And just talking, no matter the subject, is a tonic isn't it?"

"Yes," Roland said. "Very much."

"So, the funeral arrangements—are they satisfactory?"

"The arrangements are in order."

"Good, good."

They went silent then, and during the silence Rev. Price felt an urge to stand from his chair and go to Roland—go to him as one human goes to another who is alone and in pain and . . . and do what? He didn't know what. How does one human go to another? Why? He leaned forward, holding out both hands, palms turned upwards. "Roland," he said. "I don't think I'm saying anything helpful. I'm sorry. I truly want to help. What do you need? Tell me what you need."

"Everything's different now of course," Roland said. "It's all changed."

"Yes," the reverend said, relaxing back into his chair. "It must be terribly confusing. I drove by your house this morning and thought—, It's the same house but utterly different. The rocking chair is gone."

"I brought it in last night," Roland said. "I've already changed quite a bit in that house. But the fact is, I want to talk with you about something else. I was thinking . . ." Roland paused and cleared his throat. "I was thinking about a big change."

"Will you sell the house now there's only you?"

"The house is paid for. The house is comfortable."

"Well then. What change?"

"I'm thinking about getting out more."

"A good idea. You should."

"Getting out but not keeping the getting out to myself."

Rev. Price nodded. "The older generation were strict, weren't they? It was all they knew."

"What do you think about secrets, Reverend?"

"Secrets?"

"The secrets we're forced to keep."

Rev. Price looked out the window to the sidewalk and the street. A teenage boy and girl in jean jackets and blue jeans walked by, holding hands. Did the boy's parents know? he wondered. Did *her* parents know? Did they care that these two walked together, holding hands? *Secrets*—an odd word, full of hissing. He thought of the dog he'd seen that morning. A creature without secrets, without boundaries or restraint. He removed his glasses and polished them with a pocket-handkerchief. He was far-sighted, so when he glanced at Roland without glasses, he saw an indistinct blur that could have been anyone arrived to his office for advice or consolation. But it wasn't anyone, it was Roland, with something to say, perhaps something to ask. He was changing his life. He would no longer be the same person. That thought infused Rev. Price with a sudden and complete sadness.

"There can be reasons to keep secrets," he said to Roland, sliding his glasses back on. "We all require boundaries to live our lives. And boundaries are, in their way, also secrets. But if they're kept too strictly and too long, they become—I have to say—they become . . . *poisonous* is the word. Especially in families."

"I agree," Roland said. He tugged the left cuff of his blazer, crossed and re-crossed his legs. He peered out the same window through which the reverend had seen the teenage couple.

"Is there something you'd like to tell me, Roland?"

"There is. I believe I've fallen in love."

Rev. Price attempted a smile. "Love is a joyful thing," he said. "It shouldn't be kept secret."

"It shouldn't," Roland said. "But it must."

"Did you feel that while your grandmother lived, you couldn't . . . well, couldn't pursue love?"

"Not pursue, exactly. Couldn't tell."

"Does her family know?"

Roland shook his head. "His family," he said, softly. Then, louder, "His family does not know."

Rev. Price almost asked Roland to repeat what he'd said. But of course he had heard correctly.

"*His* family? I see. This is not what I expected. Of course, I cannot approve. Not at all. Have you told this person your feelings?"

"I don't believe so," Roland said. "I'm not sure."

"You're telling me this now because your grandmother has passed?"

"I suppose that's true."

"Will you tell him directly?"

"That's what I'm here to talk about. You should understand," Roland continued, "that I've been involved with rather a lot of others, since college. During college in fact. And earlier. I might as well be completely honest. But this one is . . . different. Entirely different."

"How many others, Roland?"

"I'd rather not say."

"Is he single?"

"Married. Many of the others were married—that's how it is, you know."

Rev. Price took a deep breath, holding it for a moment then releasing it through pursed lips.

"I don't know, do I? I know nothing of what you're speaking. What do you want from me Roland? I thought you wanted to talk about your grandmother's passing. Now you're raising an entirely different subject. You know I cannot condone a homosexual relationship. Is he happily married?"

"According to appearances, but appearances are deceiving. Almost always deceiving, I would say. I mean, what did my appearance tell you?"

"Does this person have children?"

"A son."

"Listen, Roland. I said that keeping secrets can be unhealthy. But in this case, telling a man with a family that you have these . . . these feelings will be traumatic—for him and for you. Certainly for his family. There will be consequences. And you must understand that in a marriage, intimacy is not the point. Of course it's welcome, and necessary for children. But many marriages do without intimacy. They do without for the sake of the marriage. The man you are referring to may be doing without for the sake of his marriage. That does not mean . . . it does not mean he needs to be confronted with your . . . feelings. All the order in his life might then be disordered. No, it would be destroyed."

"He's understanding. I believe he would want to know. Shouldn't I be honest? You yourself said that secrecy is poisonous. That was your word, *poisonous*. And it's not as if . . . as if he's a stranger."

"No," Rev. Price said. "You should *not* be honest. Not in this case. My advice is that you never speak of this to anyone. You can have such feelings and not act on them, or not act on them with certainty."

"Not act on them with certainty?"

"Yes, that's right."

"You're entirely sure?"

"I am."

"And should I remain within your congregation?"

"That would be your decision. I hope you will, of course."

Rev. Price stood, and Roland stood a moment later, buttoning the middle button of his blazer as if he'd concluded a business meeting.

"It's difficult to understand what you don't know, isn't it, Reverend?" Roland said as he opened the door. "Difficult to imagine what's outside the confines of a box."

"I don't live in a box, Roland."

"My grandmother did. And now she's released, thank God. And I'm released too. I wish you could be."

"No." Rev. Price shook his head. "No."

WHEN ROLAND HAD LEFT, Rev. Price walked to a window and opened it. He scanned for the couple he'd seen earlier but an old man holding the arm of a young woman for support walked slowly by instead.

Rev. Price briskly made his way to the tiny, windowless bathroom in the hall, flicked the light switch, shut and locked the door. He pressed his forehead against the closed door for a moment, then removed his glasses, washed his hands, splashed cold water on his face. He stared at his blurred face in the mirror: the oval shape, the curve of dark eyebrows, black hair parted on the left and combed off his forehead. He knew that others thought him to be good-looking—a handsome minister. He'd been warned at his ordination that unless he married, women in his congregation would make his life difficult. "You're a temptation," he was told. And so he married. And so he fathered a son. He became a man defined by boundaries. Good boundaries, clear boundaries. But now, here, in this small windowless room he could be anyone, or no one. The eyes, the nose, the mouth—what made his face identifiable to others and to himself—these didn't belong to him at that moment. Seen this way he could easily be Roland, blurred in the chair in his office.

He put his glasses back on. But as soon as he saw himself clearly in the mirror, he turned away, angry.

"A box," he said aloud, opening the door. "How dare he say that. How dare he say that to me."

Seer

WHEN OWEN PROSSER walked out of Thom McAn's Shoes at the end of the work week, he let his facial muscles slacken, his smile droop, his jaw unclench. He let go of his salesman face. He remembered that as a boy he would sometimes pull the corners of his eyes up or down to be a Chinaman or a sad person, or twist his lips into an old man's grimace—and walk around the house like that, talking to his parents and sister with his fake face as if everything was normal. His mother would order him to stop because one day the pretend face would stick and forever be his real face. Is that what he really wanted? And he did stop—at least until she was out of sight.

At home after work, Owen would put on his father-and-husband face, which was tight, stern, and judgmental. With this face on, Owen would await his dinner.

IT WAS NIGEL who'd pushed hardest for a family trip to the carnival in the city park. Earlier that week the boy had seen the Ferris wheel lit up like a Christmas tree, turning slow, miraculous circles during early evening, and he'd begged and cajoled his father for a family day at the carnival ever since. "Kids at school are going. Kids from church are going. And you'll have fun too, you will. Even Mam will have fun. It's better than the Shriner's Circus. Everything is fun at the carnival." Alice, a year older than Nigel, affected disinterest, but Owen knew from how she cocked her head and paid covert attention that she hoped they'd be going.

"What do you think, Owen?" his wife had asked. "It's only once a year, and I could buy Christmas presents cheap at the booths."

"Would you cut off your hand," Owen said, "because you had the opportunity once a year? And you," he said to his son, "are you a sheep following the herd over a cliff?"

"I don't think so," Nigel said.

"I don't *think* so," Owen said. "I don't *think* so."

In fact, Owen had already decided that the family would go to the carnival on Saturday—he was looking forward to it. His wife would shepherd Alice and Nigel to the rides and snack booths, and the shooting and throwing games on the midway, leaving him to wander among the alleys and corridors. Alone. It was a chance to free himself from the obligations of a family man, parishioner, shoe salesman with no prospects—and not just for an hour but an entire afternoon. It was a chance to experience something of the world beyond his house, Thom McAn's, Bethesda church, and his ever-present wife and children.

WHILE HIS WIFE queued up with Alice and Nigel for the Tilt-a-Whirl, Owen headed to the curiosity exhibits and freak shows at the carnival's outer rim, where the walkways were narrower and no one picked up the trash, which now included beer cans and pint liquor bottles. He felt lighter and taller as he strode past barkers pitching for the two-headed girl, the bearded lady, the boy with five nipples, the eighteen-inch man, the fire eater. Owen had, of course, heard rumors of these and other curiosities of the human condition, though he'd never seen one in the flesh. Could you touch one of the five nipples? Or tug the hair on the lady's chin? He felt man-of-the-world enough to recognize that most of these specimens were fakes. You pay a dollar to a con artist to see a strange person pretending to be a different sort of strange person. But some, he reasoned, slowing his pace, some might be real—men and women whose bizarre talents and afflictions made it impossible for them to raise a family, sit in a pew in church, make small talk, or hold a normal job. He knew that dwarves, for example, were authentic— one even attended his church, outfitted in a suit made for a child, all of him small except his oddly ordinary head. Yes, Owen thought, the only face a freak can wear is his own.

It was refreshing for Owen to find himself at the center of so much attention as the desperate barkers and peddlers shouted and gestured at him. But he kept walking at a slow, steady pace, noting and judging each stall or tent, each shouting face. Then one barker at a podium of stacked crates caused Owen to pause and listen. He was more elegantly dressed than the others, with a white shirt and bolo tie with silver clasp, black wing tips polished to a glossy sheen, white gloves, and a black-and-white-striped sports coat that, if you ignored the frayed cuffs, looked new. He was examining a smudge on one glove, unconcerned with the noise around him. Then he closed his eyes, thrust out his chest, and started in.

"Ladies and gentlemen, one and all," the barker announced, his strangely soft voice cutting through competing pitches. "Today only, for one dollar you may be allowed a personal audience with the Seer on his grand tour. One person at a time, if you dare, just you and he, a *tête-à-tête* that will change your life, that will irradiate your hidden self and detonate your darkest secrets. The Seer will say things you never expected—and never wanted—to hear." Now the barker's voice took on urgency. "The past! The present! The future! Do not enter the Seer's Lair if you suffer from heart disease, seizures, strokes, recurrent nightmares, or elevated blood pressure.

In such cases we will not accept your dollar. Keep your dollar and save your life. Do not enter if you are content with yourself. Do not enter if your children love you to distraction. Only the hale of body and mind, if you please!"

Although Owen was among a dozen attentive spectators, the barker turned directly to him, looking him in the eyes. "How about you, sir?" he said. "You're a man of the world. A man of substance. Are you prepared for the adventure of a lifetime? Is it worth a dollar to see your dreams—or your nightmares—take shape?"

THE LAIR WAS MUSTY AND DARK, dimly lit by a white candle melted onto a rickety knotty-pine table, a canvas folding chair set at either side. Behind one chair stood a man—humpbacked, wiry, short, with greasy grayish hair combed back over his head, dressed in an open-necked plaid shirt and loose woolen trousers, his heavy-lidded eyes half closed. The candlelight turned his skin a sickly yellow. His mouth sagged on one side, as if made of rubber.

There was no attendant to advise Owen, no instructions anywhere. But since one chair had been positioned opposite the humpback, Owen sat on it. The man nodded, slowly, as if Owen had asked a question, then abruptly sat in the other chair, his arms hanging limp at his sides. Owen looked around at boxes stacked against the canvas of the shadow-filled tent. It seemed more a shabby storage tent than a mysterious Seer's Lair. He expected something to happen, someone to walk into the room and start the show. But no one arrived.

"So what do you do?" Owen asked, finally. "What's the trick? Are you the Seer? What is it you're supposed to see?"

"What do *you* do?" the man said.

"I'm a shoe salesman," Owen replied. "Not just a salesman. In fact, I own the store." Owen justified the lie as a test for the Seer.

"I'm a shoe salesman," the man said in roughly the same tone of voice.

"You're not," Owen said. "You work in a side show." He smiled and gazed around. "A rather sad side show."

"You're not," the man said. "You work in a side show. A rather sad side show." He'd acquired a slight north Welsh accent, a parody of Owen's own. The man smiled at Owen, though his eyes were glassy and unfocused.

"What do you think you're doing?" Owen said. "What's this about? Are you really who you say you are?"

"What do you think you're doing?" the man said. "What's this about? Are you really who you say you are?"

"This isn't funny," Owen said. "If you think you're being funny, you're not."

"This isn't funny," the man said. "If you think you're being funny, you're not."

"That's it?" Owen was incredulous. "You repeat what I say? That's the whole show? That's what I paid a dollar for, a child's game? A stupid joke? You're no Seer. You're a fake. A simple-minded fake. At least other fakes have a point to them. I'm leaving, and I'm getting my money back."

"You're a fake," the man said, his Welsh accent becoming more pronounced and precise. "A simple-minded fake. At least other fakes have a point to them."

Owen stood from his chair. "Listen, you hideous humpback, I'm going to report you, do you hear? You repeat what I say one more time and I'll . . . I won't report you—I'll smack your horrible mouth so hard you won't be saying anything to anyone again. I've had all I can take from you."

The Seer was silent. He blinked once, slowly. He seemed bored. He yawned. Then he stood. He took a breath and exhaled through pursed lips.

"Your horrible mouth," he said, leaning toward Owen, his palms flat on the table. "Your horrible, horrible mouth."

At that moment the Seer twisted his lips, so his mouth took on the thin-lipped shape of Owen's mouth.

"You bastard!" Owen shouted. "You lousy bastard! I'm not joking. Keep it up and you'll get what you deserve."

"You lousy bastard," the Seer said, speaking softly, without emphasis. "You lousy, lousy bastard."

Owen felt rage erupt and churn inside him. Rage at this charlatan who stole his money and mocked him with his own words. Rage at his daily humiliations at work. Rage at the loveless marriage and pathetic children that had trapped him for life. But now, at long last, he could vent his rage.

"You'll get what you deserve," the Seer told him. "Because you're a lousy bastard."

Owen made a fist and cocked his arm to punch the face that had become his own, to split open the too-familiar lips, pop out teeth that were his teeth—dingy, crooked on the bottom. That face needed to be damaged beyond repair. But a hand took hold of Owen's wrist from behind.

"You're done," a gravelly voice announced. "You're all finished here. You've seen all you can see."

Owen turned to face a huge man in a shabby tuxedo, reeking of sweet cologne. He was completely bald, and a bulging red scar ran from his cheek to his neck.

"You get an attitude, then you're done. That's how it goes." His grip was so tight Owen's fingers began to tingle.

"But he's a cheat," Owen said. "He's no Seer. He says what you say. He pretends he's you. But it's all fake. He's not me. Don't you understand that? I want to report him."

"You're done," the huge man said, as if those words explained everything. He let go of Owen's wrist and clamped his hand—heavy as a brick—on Owen's shoulder. "This way out." He shoved Owen toward the rear of the tent.

As Owen stumbled forward, he craned his head around for a last look.

Though still dressed in a plaid shirt and woolen trousers, the Seer had grown taller. His back had straightened, the hump had melted away. Illuminated by flickering candlelight, his mouth had twisted to a knowing smile.

The Moving of the Water

MRS. ANWEN BEVAN, retired administrative assistant to a vice president in the Utica Mutual Insurance Co., devoted a portion of each day to strategizing about her yard. It was rectangular, fifty feet wide and eighty feet long, hemmed in by the yards of three neighbors. To the left and right, chain-link fences ran the length of her property. Between these, at the far end, was a ramshackle low stone wall, remnant of an early era of wall- and fence-making in this neighborhood. Mrs. Bevan did not want her yard to be overrun with trees, flowers, and vegetables, or serve as a haven for birds, insects, bees, or squirrels, as was the case with the Cavallo family on her left. She did not want her yard to harbor the detritus of children, as with the Wasilewskis on her right. Three boys played in that yard every afternoon, trudging muddy sneakers at dinnertime up the stairs to the small back porch, leaving in their wake all manner of balls, bats, bicycles, jackets, toy guns, even a half-assembled soapbox car—which remained half-assembled for a good three years before Mr. Wasilewski dragged it to the curb for the trash pickup. Mrs. Bevan had as little to do with children as could be managed. She'd been an only child in the north Wales village of Ffestiniog, and the cousins her age had emigrated with their families to London when she was a toddler. Children rarely ventured into her presence, or she into theirs.

No, she would not keep a yard intruded upon by children. She also would not allow her yard to resemble the Shank property beyond the stone wall, a wasteland of uncut grass as wispy and inconsequential as what sprouts from an old man's head, with a mini-forest of sun-starved saplings and a mound of old tires stacked against a garage, slowly melting into themselves and accommodating, she had no doubt, extended families of rodents. Mrs. Bevan had not seen Mr. Shank for many years. She'd heard he'd been ill and confined to his house—his neighbor, Mrs. Morgan, had reported on three occasions that he had in fact died: in his sleep, at his breakfast table, on the toilet, though these reports proved premature. Mrs. Bevan had also heard that Mr. Shank's grandson brought groceries and medicine to his home. At least the boy made himself useful. But Mrs. Bevan was not impressed with other members of the Shank clan. That boy's father had abandoned his family in a most peculiar manner. According to Blodwen Richards, he'd gotten into his car on a Saturday morning for grocery shopping and, after completing the errand, drove in a direction opposite from his home. His errand advanced him into a new life, without wife, child, church, or community. The boy's mother, by all accounts, turned to religion for consolation. That was all well and good, but she attended Our Lady of Lourdes several times every day—a schedule apparently acceptable in the Roman Catholic world. Would she not run out of things to say, Mrs. Bevan wondered, to her priest or to her God? And was it not odd to name a place of worship after a city in France? All in all, Mrs. Bevan thought, the Shank extended family represented a sorry state of affairs, a lesson for those willing to learn.

Mrs. Bevan observed the goings on in her immediate neighbors' yards from a bay window in her kitchen, one pane facing the Cavallo yard and another, the Wasilewskis. The middle pane overlooked her own property and the Shank property beyond. Mrs. Bevan's yard was spare but well-cared-for. She paid

Rev. Price's son to mow it once a week. She herself weeded every Saturday. She tolerated no flowers, shrubs, or trees—the last of which must one day topple upon one's house or fence. She could not abide bird feeders because they attract squirrels, a species of rodent. And birds themselves, of course, foul the very trays from which they feed. The largest yard project Mrs. Bevan had ever organized was the chainsawing of a mature sugar maple where her lawn abutted the Shank wasteland—the mother tree and fountainhead, she had no doubt, of the stunted sapling forest, as well as shelter for multitudinous birds Mrs. Bevan could hear squawking, as they will, every sunrise, every sunset.

MRS. BEVAN did not appreciate the annual spring eruption of Mr. Cavallo's flowerbeds and vegetable gardens or the irksome bustle of his late summer harvesting—his carrying back and forth, with extravagant care, wicker baskets of tomatoes and cucumbers, as if they were his newborns. But however much the profusion of his garden affronted Mrs. Bevan, she most of all resented the compost heap behind his garage, a few feet from her property. She had convinced herself that on summer afternoons she could smell the food scraps Mr. Cavallo added to his heap each evening with the fling of a bucket. One afternoon she walked to the end of the yard to inspect his compost and discovered a squirrel squatting at the very pinnacle, making a meal of carrot peels and wilted lettuce. The creature cast a malevolent glance at her and resumed its dinner.

During the years of living with Mr. Bevan, she did not think much about the Cavallo compost, but on a summer evening after the washing up she would occasionally pause from the latest issue of *Y Drych*, or from letters arriving from her cousins in London, or perhaps from a book of religious verse, and raise her nose, saying in Welsh, "Edwin, do you smell that?"

Her husband, watching television, would sleepily respond, also in Welsh, "Smell what, my dear?"

"Something on the air."

"The windows are closed, my dear," he'd say.

"It's the Cavallo compost," she'd say, switching to English. "It seeps into the house. It *permeates*, you see."

Mrs. Bevan had an instinctual grasp of English, more extensive, more sure (though delivered rather stiffly), than her husband, who was fully fluent only when speaking Welsh to friends from the north of Wales.

"Ah yes," he'd reply. "Of course it does. Of course. Yes. 'Permeates,' as you say."

He'd return to his program and she to her reading.

Edwin had been widowed five years before proposing marriage to her. It all happened rather quickly. One Sunday when they were chatting after the service, he walked with her to the apartment she rented three blocks from Bethesda. He then formed a habit of walking her home each Sunday, and she found she enjoyed his company. Early on they mostly talked about his deceased wife, and his sons who were now grown men with families. His eldest wanted him to sell his house on Storrs Avenue and move in with his family in West Winfield, twenty miles south of the city. But then he couldn't attend the Bethesda service on Sundays—and he wasn't yet ready for that change. Soon their conversation moved from the past to their present lives. And one day, after they'd stepped on to her front porch, he took hold of her hand, and proposed—a turn of events that surprised everyone, herself included. It was a very formal proposal, in Welsh of course, and she accepted, right there on the porch, without really thinking. Why? she'd wondered many times since. It was so unlike her usual way of proceeding with decisions. But somehow she knew—without fully knowing the man—that he was a good man. And she was right: theirs proved a good marriage, far better than she could have imagined, despite their many differences, despite the chilly reception given her by Edwin's sons and their wives and children. She moved into Edwin's house to discover that he was easy-going. He enjoyed neighbors, made a point of chatting, and to be neighborly chose to weed the yard while Mr. Cavallo was tending his vegetable garden on a Saturday afternoon.

The day Mrs. Bevan learned of Edwin's cancer—that was a terrible day. Early on it was difficult to believe anything was wrong with her husband besides shortness of breath and a cough that worsened when he lay down in bed. How she bore the diagnosis from Dr. Evans and managed those last months of steep decline, how she survived the funeral and the weeks and years that followed, she could not say. But she did survive. She made a point of surviving. And she didn't weep in public—not once, though Edwin's sons and their wives and children carried on at the funeral and committal as if they were Irish or Italian, handkerchiefs wiping reddened eyes and clearing blubbering noses. For Edwin, she maintained her dignity. For Edwin, she demonstrated undiminished strength. But since his death, she'd found life to be a far darker journey.

IT WAS IN EARLY SEPTEMBER, two years after Edwin's passing, that Mrs. Bevan paid the Cavallos a visit to address the issue of the compost. They invited her into their sitting room, which Mrs. Bevan observed was spotless, with a formal, old-world feel—not dissimilar to her own front parlor. Mr. Cavallo was dressed casually, in wrinkle-free dark trousers and a light green shirt. Mrs. Cavallo brought in a pot of coffee with delicate china cups and saucers, a bowl of sugar cubes, and a plate of homemade biscotti. When all had been served, Mrs. Bevan went to the point.

"Mr. Cavallo," she said. "That heap behind your garage. It has an odor."

"My compost?"

"Yes, that."

"I've kept a compost since, well, since we moved here twenty-three years ago. You've never mentioned an odor before. Your husband and I had a thousand conversations, with him weeding and me turning compost."

"It's garbage," she said. "Plain and simple."

"It is not," Mr. Cavallo said, leaning forward. "I compost only vegetable scraps. I mix those with soil and leaves. I water it daily. I turn it over weekly. It's hot as an oven in my compost, so nothing can smell."

"Vermin and such," Mrs. Bevan said, "seek out garbage."

"There's never been a rat in my yard," Mr. Cavallo said. "Or that I've seen in this neighborhood. And I need that compost for my tomato and basil plants." He paused and leaned back. "Isabella," he said, "would you bring the basket from the kitchen? The one I prepared."

"Nothing in this world," he said to Mrs. Bevan, "is more pleasing for me than digging compost for my garden. It is rich and clean. That's why we eat so well." He smiled and patted his ample waistline as his wife reappeared with an oval wicker basket heaped with ripe tomatoes. "These are for you, Mrs. Bevan," he said, gesturing to the basket. "They make the best sauce in the world. After tasting these you will shun other tomatoes." He paused dramatically. "And there are more where those came from."

"I cannot eat tomatoes or a sauce made of them," Mrs. Bevan said. "Because of acid indigestion."

Mr. Cavallo could only stare at her. He turned to his wife and erupted into rapid, sharpish Italian.

Mrs. Bevan rose from her chair. "I will see myself to the door," she said. "If you would simply remove that heap, please, at your earliest convenience."

THE NEXT SUNDAY AFTERNOON Mr. Cavallo spent an hour transferring the compost pile, wheelbarrow after wheelbarrow, to the opposite side of his yard—a space previously devoted to potatoes. Where the heap had been, Mr. Cavallo set a basket of tomatoes—the same he'd tried to give to Mrs. Bevan. What on earth? she thought when seeing it the next morning. Hadn't he understood the words *acid indigestion*? Then she realized that the basket was not a gift but a reproach. She resolved to think no more about it.

A WEEK AFTER her success with the Cavallos, Mrs. Bevan sat at the table by her bay window watching Mr. Wasilewski walk from his garage to his back yard with a long-handled spade, then return a minute later with a wheelbarrow. He commenced digging. And each day, following his arrival home from work, Mrs. Bevan watched him dig steadily for an hour, sometimes alone, sometimes with one or more sons, shovelful upon shovelful, wheelbarrow upon wheelbarrow, the earth carted to an expanding hill at the bottom of his yard. Why, she wondered, does he want to create a hill in his yard? Or is the hole in the ground the point? The sons worked silently and—she thought—sullenly, though the father was bumptious, singing rough-sounding songs in Polish, telling jokes to his sons that she couldn't pretend to understand—and had no interest in understanding. To study these activities, Mrs. Bevan bought a pair of binoculars at Yancy's Hardware. Soon she was cataloguing each stage of the Wasilewski project in a small notebook.

On a Saturday afternoon, Mrs. Bevan watched Mr. Wasilewski line the hole with black plastic, then fill it with water from a hose.

When the water rose high enough, he carried a bucket from his garage to the hole. What he dumped in was more water, with flashes of wriggling orange lumps. Fish! Mrs. Bevan stood from her chair by the bay window. Orange fish would live in that hole. And in due course, no doubt, frogs. And turtles. And insects. Birds might drop from the sky for a bath and drink from the same fouled water. And creatures would breed in that hole, Mrs. Bevan supposed, because standing water, as is well documented, soon becomes a cesspool of breeding. Mosquitoes would hatch eggs there, no doubt. That had to be Mr. Wasilewski's purpose—to breed creatures and sell the spawn to those trafficking in such things. Why else create such a disgusting water hole in a yard? But to breed and sell creatures, she further reasoned, even in America must require a license. She'd heard about a family down the block, the DeStefanos, who'd been fined by a judge for breeding pit bull fighting dogs in their basement. The dogs were blind, she'd heard, from never glimpsing the sun, and deaf from never hearing a kind word.

So Mrs. Anwen Bevan visited Jock Wasilewski the next afternoon. His wife was not at home, and Mr. Wasilewski did not offer coffee or a biscuit. He led Mrs. Bevan into the TV room, where they sat on red vinyl chairs on either side of a light brown card table. Landscapes that Mrs. Bevan assumed had been cut out of a calendar were scotch-taped in a vertical line on one wall: a cathedral, a castle, a mountain hut with a few goats standing nearby. These were the only decorations in the room. On the card table was a well-used deck of cards; stacks of red, white, and blue poker chips; and a half full bottle of Budweiser. The TV was on—a baseball game, which Mr. Wasilewski did not turn off.

"I'm glad you stopped by," Jock Wasilewski said. "I don't think we've exchanged more than four words all year. 'Good morning'—I said that once. And maybe 'Good evening,' though I'm not sure."

"You have fabricated a water hole," she told him. "In your yard."

"You noticed," he said. "Yes, it was a lot of work, but worth it I hope." After a quick glance at the TV, he added, "It's a pond."

"I know what it is, and I would like you to fill it in."

"What's that?"

"I would like you to fill in that hole."

"Why would I put back in what I spent a week digging out?"

"Because," she said, "we live in a city, not the wilderness. There are no Red Indians here. If you wish to live in the wilderness, you must relocate."

"The pond is on private property—my property."

Mrs. Bevan tightened her lips. "There are rules, Mr. . . . Mr. Wasilewski, even for private property. This is not Sodom; neither is it Gomorrah. You cannot run a business in your yard without a proper license."

"A license?"

"A license for fish breeding. Or frog breeding. No matter which. Have you not heard of the plagues of frogs, gnats, and flies?"

Then Mr. Wasilewski laughed. He laughed long and loud. While he laughed, Mrs. Bevan did not change her expression, which was stern, and pinched.

"Biblical pestilence," she said, "should not be scoffed at."

"Do you know where I work, Mrs. Bevan?" he asked.

"I do not."

"I make sausages at Hapanowicz's." He held up two meaty, calloused hands. "I work at a grinder. It's messy. It smells bad— the smell doesn't go away when you leave work or even after a bath. I come home at half past five and my wife does not welcome me because she's not at home—she cleans the homes of rich people along the Parkway, the ones with big front lawns and grand entrances. Who got them the money for those houses? The men who dug the canals, that's who, the Irish and the Polish. Dug the ditches that filled with water, and then the money flowed in. Do you know what I want when I'm home, Mrs. Beven? What I want is to drink a beer and sit by water. I love water. In Poland my family lived near a lake by the chemical plant where my father worked. The lake smelled as if something large in it had died. We couldn't swim in that lake. Couldn't fish it—fish could not survive in that water. But I didn't care. My family picnicked on the stony shore—my parents, two brothers, three sisters. As a child I dreamed of living by a lake when I was a man, a clean lake with no bad smell. I've never entered a swimming pool. I've only seen the ocean through a porthole on the ship that brought me here. So I dug out that pond with these hands. Now, I have water on my own property. Clean water with living fish. It's not for breeding. It's not for my children or my wife. It's for me. It's something I made with these Polish butcher's hands, to sit next to, and look at."

"You must now use those impressive hands," Mrs. Bevan said, "to fill in that hole."

"I will not."

Mrs. Bevan removed her notebook from her purse. "I hoped it would not come to this," she said. "But you leave me no choice. I have documented everything that you've done to create that hole. The authorities might be interested."

"They might be," Mr. Wasilewski said. "Or not." He paused. "May I ask you something, Mrs. Bevan?"

"If it's not impolite."

"When did you come to this country?"

"My parents and I arrived in nineteen hundred and nine."

"I see. I arrived much later, but we have that in common, coming to this country. I've lived here since I was seventeen. Now I'm thirty-one. I have a wife and three sons. I think I know what I can or cannot do. In this country, I can have a pond in my backyard if I want. I am sorry that you object."

"It's all so . . ." Mrs. Bevan couldn't find the words. She started to tear up, and tugged a white handkerchief from the sleeve of her blue dress, pressing it against her eyes. "It's so . . . terrible."

Mr. Wasilewski smiled. "Water is relaxing, Mrs. Bevan," he said. "And refreshing. We need it, don't we? We crawled out of it when we weren't humans, or so I've heard. Priests sprinkle water on the heads of babies, do they not?"

"Are you a Catholic, Mr. Wasilewski?" Mrs. Bevan asked as she returned her notebook to her purse.

"Jewish, if you go back far enough, then Catholic, but that's a long story. Now I'm pagan."

Mrs. Bevan said nothing.

"You can visit me in my yard any time. We'll sit together by the pond. You'll have a cup of tea. That's what the Welsh drink, isn't it? I'll drink beer. We'll talk. And we'll look at what's around us. The world, Mrs. Bevan, is all around us."

HAVING SUFFERED DEFEAT at the hands of Jock Wasilewski, Mrs. Bevan walked stiffly back to her house, her purse wedged under an arm. She was upset that a man had seen her wipe tears from her eyes. She didn't understand how that could have happened. She didn't cry at Edwin's funeral, yet teared up when talking to a boor about his water hole. Of course she'd never visit that man again, never enter his ramshackle yard, never sit next to him as he drank alcohol and stared at water. It was all preposterous.

Mrs. Bevan put a kettle on the stove for tea, and when she had poured a cup and stirred in the milk and sugar, she thought again about her yard. She was only now getting used to the absence of the maple tree she'd had cut down the previous month—that tree had masked the crumbling dry-stone wall separating her yard from Mr. Shank's. Was it possible that she'd made a mistake? With the maple tree gone, those ugly stones were all she could see. They reminded her of the walls dissecting the hills near Ffestiniog: disheveled, snaking shapes that held nothing in, kept nothing out, yet demanded attention nevertheless. The Shank wall was similarly primitive, unruly, unsightly, punctuated with gaps anyone might walk through—but she could not have the stones carted away because they lay wholly on his property.

Then she saw something that exponentially intensified her dislike of the wall. Birds. Birds had settled on the stones. Sparrows, to be exact. A plague of sparrows. She did not remember ever seeing birds on the wall before. Perhaps her eye had been distracted by the now absent maple. Over the following week she pondered how these sparrows might be prevented from congregating there, squawking and defecating and disrupting. They always faced the Shank house, turning their collective feathery backs upon her property. One morning she observed a sparrow leap off the wall then swoop to resettle back where it had perched—and thus she came upon the solution. Birds, like humans, have feet.

Later that same day, Mrs. Bevan emptied a box of thumb-tacks in a stream across the stones, shooing away sparrows as she walked, grimly shaking out the last tacks upon the last tumble down stones. Close up, the stones were more disturbing than she'd suspected: irregular and primeval, mottled with lichen and moss, with overlapped splatterings of bird feces. Mrs. Bevan hoped that five hundred sharp points would repel even creatures as tenacious in their bad habits as sparrows.

THE FOLLOWING WEDNESDAY Mrs. Bevan's phone rang shortly after nine while she was washing breakfast dishes.

"I've been in hospital," Mr. Shank said after introducing himself. "For three weeks."

"Well, well," Mrs. Bevan said, "I'm sorry to hear that."

He let loose a cough muffled by a handkerchief.

"I rarely get out," he said. "Truth be told I am . . . I am not well. But I saw from my bedroom window that my birds no longer sit on my wall. I asked my grandson to investigate—he's a good boy who does whatever I ask—and he said nails had been scattered across the stones."

"They are thumbtacks, not nails."

"Whatever they are, they are not good for birds."

"That's the point, Mr. Shank. I have done us a favor."

He coughed longer and more violently than before.

"They're my birds," he said.

"Nonsense," Mrs. Bevan said. "They are wild creatures. They belong to no person. They do as they please."

"I feed them," he said. "They wait for me to fill the feeder. I in turn wait for them. I enjoy them. It's my grandson who feeds them now, since I've been ill, but in any event they expect to be fed. Since you had their tree cut down, they have no branches on which to perch. But they continue to eat from my feeder and now must sit on my wall. And I spend a considerable part of every day watching them from my bedroom window.

"I am not responsible," said Mrs. Bevan, "for wild birds."

"This afternoon my grandson will pick off every nail you set on the wall. I am asking you, please, no more nails. That wall," he added, solemnly, "is on my property."

And with that he'd made a point Mrs. Bevan could not refute.

THAT AFTERNOON Mrs. Beven hired Alexander Pappas, a carpenter, to construct a fence to block her view of the Shank property: the stone wall, the yard, and the broken-down house beyond. This fence would run in front of the Shank stones, meeting the chain-link fences on the Cavallo and Wasilewski properties, thus enclosing her yard on three sides. Mr. Pappas carted into her yard the necessary posts, boards, nails, concrete mix, a bucket, a shovel, and a post-hole digger. He sunk the corner posts deeply into concrete. After waiting two days for the concrete to set, he screwed—not nailed—the vertical boards of thick cedar to the posts, starting at the Wasilewski yard and working toward the Cavallo property. It was an excellent fence.

"The fence should now be stained," Mr. Pappas said. "You might give that job to a neighborhood boy, who'll charge less than me."

"I do think you charged rather much for this bit of fence," Mrs. Bevan informed Mr. Pappas as she wrote out the check.

JUST AFTER she'd set on her kitchen table a pot of tea, a plate with buttered toast, and a boiled egg in its eggcup, Mrs. Bevan was shocked to see a red-haired boy, thin, perhaps ten or eleven, dash out from her driveway into her yard. He wore a red plaid shirt, tail hanging out, and jeans with pant legs too short, exposing white socks and pale calves above red sneakers. He stopped in the middle of the yard, gazing around as if he'd never seen a back yard before. It occurred to Mrs. Bevan that perhaps he'd never seen one as well kept as hers. That notion was followed by a surge of indignation that a boy would presume to trespass onto her property. Then Mrs. Bevan remembered her new fence. The boy could not in fact continue on through her yard, as there was no exit. What would he do? What *could* he do, when confronted with sturdy fencing anchored in concrete that had thoroughly set? He had invaded her yard and now must exit the way he arrived, having wasted time and effort. What would he learn from this experience? she asked herself. Something important about life and its limitations and frustrations? About how one should behave, even if one is as insolent as—what was the word?—as insolent as a child?

Then the boy did an incredible thing. He faced Mrs. Bevan's house, and solemnly made the sign of the cross before bolting toward the new fence. Instead of stopping short, he leapt onto it. Using gaps between boards for traction, he scaled to the top, where he straddled the fence, shot his arms into a triumphant V, and slid to the other side, all with the facility, Mrs. Bevan thought, of a trained monkey.

She was stunned. "A Catholic boy," she said aloud.

Mrs. Bevan hurried to her yard. "How dare you!" she shouted. "How dare you behave in this manner!" But she was shouting at the air. She stared at the fence in disgust. "Why?" she said aloud. "What's the point?" But when she summoned up the geography of her neighborhood, she understood why a boy would cut across her property and into the Shank yard: this was a Saturday morning, and her neighbor's yard led to a driveway that emptied into Oneida Street, across from the city park with its rusted swing set, broken merry-go-round, and an unmowed field where ragtag boys played their ragtag games with no adult supervision. A child using this route and not the sidewalks would save, perhaps, five minutes on his way to the park. An eternity for an unruly and impatient boy.

Then something caught her eye. On the grass where the boy had crossed himself was a card with words printed on it. Mrs. Bevin hesitated. Could it be one of those . . . those *disgusting* cards she'd heard about from her cousin Bea when they were girls? He was irrefutably a boy, after all. But it was not that sort of card, and the writing proved to be a prayer titled "Comfort," with select words highlighted in red. On the other side was a Jesus with arms outstretched, a bright purple heart on his chest, golden light breaking through clouds behind his head. It was, she knew, a Catholic object, offensive in its gaudy literalness. She strode into her house and set the card in a kitchen drawer, because it wasn't right to toss even a sacrilegious *Iesu Grist* into the trash.

Glancing out the bay window to her right, she saw Jock Wasilewski on a lawn chair in front of his pool, smoking. He set the cigarette on a saucer by his feet and picked up a bottle of beer.

Mrs. Bevan shook her head. "The blind, the lame, the withered," she said. "They wait for the moving of the water." She lifted her face to the heavens. *"Arglwydd, arwain trwy'r anialwch."*

MRS. BEVAN did not see the red-haired boy for the rest of the week. The following Saturday morning at seven-fifteen she made her pot of tea and soft-boiled egg and buttered bread, turned on her radio for classical music, and seated herself at the table by the bay window overlooking her yard. The boy wouldn't, she thought. He would not. He would dare not a second time.

But at a little past eight he appeared, running into her yard from the driveway. He paused halfway to the fence. He slid his hands into his pockets, leaned forward, and stared at the grass. Mrs. Bevan knew what it was he sought—the Jesus card he'd dropped. The boy took his time. He untied and retied his sneaker laces. He stood. And he did a strange thing. He pulled a paper bag from his back pocket, pouring its contents of bread crumbs into a little heap on the cropped yard grass, like an offering. He took two steps back.

A sparrow fluttered down, hopping to within a foot of the heap. It twitched its head. It retreated then hopped closer. The boy remained a statue. Another sparrow appeared, and two more. A squirrel arrived, dashing up to the heap, scattering the birds, gorging frenetically until its cheeks bulged like twin balloons. Then the boy started walking in spirals, scanning for the prayer card, turning his head oddly as he inspected the ground—very like a bird himself. More birds arrived to search for remaining crumbs. In a single fluid motion the boy whipped around and bolted towards the fence.

Mrs. Bevan stormed out to her yard only to witness the boy's leap to the other side. Not only did the fencing not deter him—it was clearly an attraction. She gripped a board with two hands and yanked. The fence could sustain ten climbing boys, and more. It was, indeed, just the thing for climbing. The entire debacle, she decided, was the fault of that Greek carpenter. Why would a man design and build a fence that was not a barrier but . . . a plaything?

As Mrs. Bevan assessed the fence from top to bottom, a flash of silver on the ground caught her eye. She picked up a round medal featuring a head framed by a halo. It had a classical, even a Grecian, look to it.

LATER THAT SATURDAY, when Mrs. Bevan was considering how best to solve the problem of the fence, her doorbell rang. Thinking it to be the newspaper boy, she brought her purse with her. So she was surprised to see on her doorstep the very same red-haired boy who had twice run into her yard and scaled her fence. And next to him, a short, bald, elderly man out of breath, as if he'd run a race, his face thin and flushed. The boy, Mrs. Bevan noted, was cross-eyed, though not precisely: one eye focused while the other roamed, which must be why he'd turned his head so oddly when searching for the dropped Jesus card. The boy appraised her with his good eye while the other eye drooped in the direction of his pug nose. A smudge of mud covered the middle of one cheek.

"Good afternoon," the old man said.

"Good afternoon."

"You don't recognize me?"

She squinted. "Is it Mr. Shank?"

"I know it's been a while—years in fact. I'm sure I'm . . . much altered." He paused, launched into a long, liquid cough, and spit into a handkerchief he pulled from his pocket then quickly stuffed back in. The boy looked away. "I don't get out much, Mrs. Bevan. Indeed, I haven't been out since my last stay at hospital."

Mrs. Bevan did not invite the pair in, thinking it best to deal with such individuals on one's doorstep.

"This is Alec," Mr. Shank said. "My grandson."

"Ah, your grandson." Mrs. Bevan examined him. "Young man," she said, "your face needs washing."

"Yes," Mr. Shank said. "He's been digging out a flowerbed for my front yard. In fact he helps me around the house every Saturday. And we . . . we didn't have time to wash up, did we Alec? His mother is expecting him."

"Yes," Mr. Shank said next, as if Mrs. Bevan had asked a question. "Yes, yes, yes. But speaking of yards, Alec has something to say. An apology, isn't that so my boy?"

"I'm sorry I cut through your yard," Alec said in a rehearsed monotone. His good eye aimed at his grandfather while the other drifted towards the sky. He crossed himself quickly and jammed the hand in his pocket.

"It was difficult to convince him to come along," Mr. Shank said, a twinkle in his eye. "He's rather afraid of you."

"Why should he be?"

"He thinks you're . . ." Mr. Shank paused. "Well, in a word, he thinks you're something of a . . . a witch you know. He saw you once, wearing a shawl and holding a broom, which to his mind proved the case. I believe you were sweeping the sidewalk." And he laughed, which quickly developed into another coughing fit. When finished, he saw that Mrs. Bevan was not smiling. "Perhaps," he said, "perhaps that's not . . . funny. Well, it's ridiculous. But you can imagine the notions boys get."

"I can imagine no such thing," she said.

"Yes, yes, well, they will have their notions I assure you. I receive two ears full of notions each time he visits."

"It was not one occasion on which this boy entered my yard," Mrs. Bevan said. "There were two."

"I know," Mr. Shank said. "I learned all this today. When Alec visits me, the boy"—Mr. Shank glanced at Alec—"the boy likes to pray to Saint Peregrine—the both of us must pray, in fact, that's the long and the short. He insists. We must get down on our knees—and I have a devil of a time getting back up, let me tell you. But I must say, I rather . . . it's rather touching. His mother's Irish and she's become a great Catholic this year. I myself am mongrel. Scots, German, Irish, some French Canadian. A citizen of the world I suppose."

"A mongrel?" Mrs. Bevan said. "I see."

"Yes, at any rate, when Alec arrived to my house this morning, he'd lost Saint Peregrine. And we always pray with that particular medal to hand. None other will do the job."

"What a shame," Mrs. Bevan said.

"He's always losing things. He'd lose his nose if it wasn't growing out of his face, wouldn't you my boy?"

Alec nodded solemnly.

"And his pockets have holes, which I have asked his mother to sew up. Quite fantastic holes. Ravenous holes. That, or else he enjoys hanging upside down. Do you Alec? Are you related to the bat?"

"No," Alec said. "I'm not."

"He also lost his prayer card. But his mother . . ." Mr. Shank paused. "Well, his mother has hundreds of those. The medal, however—there's only one medal. When I asked Alec which route he took from his mother's house to mine, thinking we might retrace his steps, he made his confession regarding your yard. And he mentioned climbing your fence. He's an honest boy, this one, and never lies."

Mrs. Bevan nodded solemnly. "The fence was not cheap," she said.

"So I told the boy he must apologize, and..." Mr. Shank slid from his "and" into another bout of coughing, closely observed by Alec's functioning eye. This time when he spat into his handkerchief Mrs. Bevan saw a flash of red.

"And I said that after he apologized, he might ask permission to search your yard as the medal must have slipped from his pocket while he was... while he was climbing your fence."

"He most certainly may not enter my yard to rummage for that object," Mrs. Bevan said. "I am a Calvinist Methodist."

"It's silver," Mr. Shank said. "In color, not true silver. It has no monetary value, but Alec tells me I cannot replace it. Children will have their ideas. It's the size of a quarter with a necklace attached, though Alec has not worn it, have you Alec?"

"Your cancer wouldn't get cured if I wore it," Alec said. "And if we used a different one, the saint would know, and it wouldn't work."

"Enough Alec," Mr. Shank said. "Mrs. Bevan doesn't require extraneous detail. In any event, I'm sure there are no such rules about the workings of saints' medals."

Mrs. Bevan let go her grip on her doorknob and took a good look at Mr. Shank. He was breathing fast, as if standing on her stoop was equivalent to running in place. His face was flushed the same meaty red as Mr. Cavallo's ripe tomatoes. But the thing that affected her most was in his eyes. She recognized it as she would a detested relative arrived unannounced. This was the look in her father's eyes after the first heart attack when she had come home early from work to find him lying on the couch, insisting nothing was wrong, though he couldn't move either arm. The second attack killed him three days later. She saw it in her mother's eyes after the stroke that silenced her— she'd sputter and gag, trying mightily to say the words she thought must be said at the end of a life—and not one could be managed. She lingered for three weeks, unable to eat or drink. And of course it was in Edwin's eyes when the pneumonia set in. With infection in Edwin's lungs, the doctor told her, she must prepare for the worst.

"We understand your position," Mr. Shank said. "But if you come across the medal, would you let me know? It would mean a great deal to Alec."

Mrs. Bevan removed the Saint Peregrine medal from her purse and held it out.

"Take it," she said to Alec. "I have no use for such a thing."

Alec shifted his good eye to his grandfather, who nodded. Then he plucked the medal from her palm, examined it, and slipped it in his pocket. He stepped away from Mrs. Bevan, as if afraid she'd try to take it back.

Mr. Shank mustered a sly look. "Thank you, Mrs. Bevan," he said, "for . . . well, for remembering."

"I am incapable of forgetting," she said. Then she added, almost as an afterthought, "You knew my husband, I believe."

"We spoke over my wall many times. At least once a week. Mr. Bevan was a great lover of stone walls—they reminded him of his childhood in north Wales, he told me. He was an old-world gentleman. I knew his first wife also—I hope you don't mind my saying this. And his sons."

Mrs. Bevan nodded. "It's difficult," she said, "to . . ." She stopped speaking and glanced at Alec, desperate to leave her witchy presence now he'd gotten back his medal.

She tried again. "It's difficult to know..." But she couldn't finish that sentence either. "Edwin," she said finally, "had a way about him. I never knew such a man."

"Yes," Mr. Shank said. "He had a way, didn't he? A very good way. A delightful way."

He turned to Alec. "My boy, we must be going. You have apologized triumphantly. You have retrieved your medal—now please don't keep it near the hole in your pocket. It's been an altogether excellent visit, and your mother is expecting you. Perhaps now she'll sew up those fantastic holes, if a needle and thread can be found."

"Thank you, Mrs. Bevan," he said. "I can guarantee that the boy will not be short-cutting through your yard again. Isn't that so Alec?"

Alec nodded.

Mr. Shank extended a hand, and Mrs. Bevan shook it.

"The boy is quite a climber of fences," she said. "Isn't he?"

"I believe so," Mr. Shank said, "though I've not seen him do so myself."

"You're good, aren't you?" she said rather sharply to Alec. "You're a clever little monkey."

"In gym," Alec said, "I pull myself up the knotted rope to the ceiling. Then I let myself down. I never fall, and no one's as fast."

"Yes," Mrs. Bevan said. "I see that. Quick. A quick boy."

"Goodbye, Mrs. Bevan," Mr. Shank said.

"Goodbye," she said.

She watched them proceed down the sidewalk, the boy holding his grandfather's hand. Mr. Shank walked slowly, with a pronounced limp, and they stopped every dozen steps so he could catch his breath. The boy talked nonstop while Mr. Shank bent his head to listen. She thought about how the two would continue in that manner to the end of the block, turn right and walk on to the next block, then right a half block further to Mr. Shank's front door. If she hadn't paid Mr. Pappas to construct that fence, they could have simply walked through her back yard and been home in less than a minute. A waste of time, she thought, all that unnecessary walking.

She watched them disappear around the corner, certain she would never see Mr. Shank again.

"There are terrible times coming," she said, as if the old man remained on her stoop. "Lonely and terrible times. For me, and for you and your devoted grandson, and your daughter-in-law, though I've not met her. You're living to a terrible end. Living with that boy's eyes as they are. Impossible to explain, or understand, why the terrible things happen, but they must. The terrible things happen, and hurt us, and go on to hurt others. Believing in a saint or not, doesn't matter, praying or not praying. Going to church three times a day, or decently once a week on the Sabbath. When it comes to terrible things, none of it matters. You'll wish that you were pulling the strings—everything would be different if you were, but you are most certainly not. Terrible how nothing you wish or feel or need makes a jot of difference when it ought to make the most difference. You think you're doing something, bringing that boy to me to apologize. The boy believes he's accomplished a wonder in retrieving his precious medal. He believes in miracles. You both believe you're making things happen. But you're not. Not the things that count.

"*Ofnadwy,*" she said aloud. "*Siwr o fod. Pethau ofnadwy.*"

The boy would be cheap to hire, she thought, to stain the fence. And Mr. Shank, for the time he has left, could be responsible for the boy's work. Fences, she thought, should not be brought low by the prejudices of weather. They're useful. They keep out creatures. They establish boundaries. They should be cared for, like all useful things. And if the boy behaved himself, he might be allowed to make his way through her yard and over the fence to his grandfather's house. And now they'd met, he'd have no reason to make that absurd sign of the cross while on her property.

His scaling of the fence, she thought, how quick, how sure. Quite amazing. As long as nothing is damaged, some arrangement might be made.

After walking into her house and settling at the table by the bay window, Mrs. Bevan's eyes locked upon Jock Wasilewski in a red fuzzy bathrobe, slouched on his frayed white-and-green lawn chair by his pond, holding a beer bottle. His bare feet rested on a plastic crate. Next to the crate were two empty bottles, and Mrs. Bevan assumed full bottles could be found in the cooler by his chair. She noted that he had large feet for a short man, and periodically wiggled his toes. His loosely cinched bathrobe exposed the curve of his belly, domed like a huge brown egg.

A robin swooped from somewhere on high and plopped at the edge of the pond. As it fluttered wings for a bath, Mr. Wasilewski leaned forward. He watched the bird drink its fill, and leap into the air.

"Baptized!" Jock Wasilewski shouted, raising his bottle. "Baptized with Wasilewski water!" He laughed heartily, open-mouthed, then leaned back to watch the bird cross Mrs. Bevan's yard on its journey west, spraying water drops as it flew.

"Hallelujah," he said more softly, wiggling his toes. "Hallelujah, and the saints be praised."

Notes on Welsh Words, Phrases, and Names

Alun: pronounced *Alin*

Arglwydd, arwain trwy'r anialwch: literally translated as *Lord, lead [me] through the wilderness*; translated as *Guide me, O thou great Jehovah* in the famous hymn sung to John Hughes's "Cwm Rhondda"

bara brith: traditional Welsh fruit bread

bach and fach: diminutives for a male and a female child

chapel/church: in Wales *chapel* refers to the building in which a nonconformist denomination worships; in the United States, Welsh Americans commonly use *church* for these buildings

Dai Siop: Dai runs a grocery shop (*siop*); as still happens in Wales, those with common surnames such as Jones or Williams might be identified by occupation

Diawl: *Devil*

eisteddfodau: Welsh cultural festival, plural

Iesu Grist: *Jesus Christ*

Duw: *God*

Llew: short for Llewelyn; *llew* also means *lion* in Welsh; the *Ll* is a voiceless lateral fricative not used in English

Nain: *Grandmother*

nos da: *good night*

Ofnadwy. Siwr o fod. Pethau ofnadwy.: *Terrible. Without doubt. Terrible things.*

Pice ar y maen: a south Wales term for *Welsh cakes*; in English, literally translated as *cakes on the stone*; in north Wales, these are called *cacennau cri*

Siân: pronounced *Shan*

Tad: *Dad*

Tada: *Daddy*

Taid: *Grandfather* (north Wales)

Twm: pronounced *Toom*

Y Drych: Welsh American newspaper